'Get out of ... flood!' Kirst ...

'You really are ... ... man, Harry Graham. We are—even I am—grateful, but if you don't want thanks then that's okay.'

He seemed taken aback—even hesitant—and when he said, 'Yes—well...' and let the end of the sentence vanish into the ether, Kirsten found that the urge to hug him had returned, although she knew full well that hugging Harry Graham would be dangerous.

'I'll try to keep in touch,' he said.

'Good luck,' Kirsten said, then, heart pounding from the onslaught of too many mixed emotions, she added, 'Stay safe.'

Harry nodded, and all but marched from the room, returning only seconds later to snap, 'And you stay safe as well. Keep away from the water. No foolish heroics. Hear me!'

Kirsten smiled, unable to ignore the tiny glow of happiness his words had lit inside her.

As she lists her hobbies as reading, reading and reading, it's hardly surprising that **Meredith Webber** fell into writing when she needed a job she could do at home. Not that anyone in the family considers it a 'real job'! She is fortunate enough to live on the Gold Coast in Queensland, Australia, as this gives her the opportunity to catch up with many other people with the same 'unreal' job when they visit the popular tourist area.

Recent titles by the same author:

TRUST ME
LOVE ME
MARRY ME
BAUBLES, BELLS AND BOOTEES

HEART'S COMMAND

BY
MEREDITH WEBBER

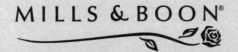

First published in Great Britain 2000
Harlequin Mills & Boon Limited,
Eton House, 18-24 Paradise Road, Richmond, Surrey TW9 1SR

© Meredith Webber 2000

ISBN 0 263 82288 5

Set in Times Roman 10½ on 11½ pt.
03-0201-50502

Printed and bound in Spain
by Litografía Rosés, S.A., Barcelona

CHAPTER ONE

'WHAT do you mean, the building's occupied?'

From within the old stone building, Kirsten heard the steely demand, the voice not so much loud as carrying. She strained to hear the reply from the young soldier, a punctiliously polite lieutenant who hadn't deserved the wrath she'd heaped on him.

Nothing.

Perhaps the army didn't teach voice projection until later in their recruits' careers.

'Squatting? Someone's squatting in there and you haven't moved them on?'

It was the carrying voice again, and she guessed the underling was being flayed by the bits she couldn't hear. In all fairness to the youth, she should step in.

Or out, in this case. At present, she was lurking in the former convent's marble-tiled entry, while the men were standing in what feeble protection from the rain the portico, formed by the first floor balcony, afforded them.

Footsteps on the front steps finessed her plan and all she had time to do was step forward, hoping it would look as if she'd just that minute walked into the foyer.

The carrying voice belonged to a tall, erect man—the phrase 'soldierly bearing' flashed obligingly through Kirsten's mind. He was so wet his army fatigues clung to him like a second skin, revealing a body of hard, flat planes and sculpted muscle. His dark-looking hair was plastered to a well-shaped skull, but the weak light from the opening behind him threw his face into shadow so she was unable to read either his expression or the colour of his eyes.

5

Beyond him, she could see large trucks pulling up, and hear orders being shouted.

'May I help you?' Kirsten asked in her carefully polite, 'talking to bureaucracy' voice.

His strides shortened as if he was taken aback to find her there—so much so he didn't reply to her directly but turned to his hapless subordinate again.

'I understood all women and children had been evacuated from the town, Lieutenant.'

His tone suggested 'exterminated' might have been an equally fitting verb.

'Not quite all,' the unfortunate, who'd introduced himself to Kirsten as Lt James Ross, replied.

'I can see that, Lieutenant!'

Not only carrying, but honed to the sharpness of a fine steel blade, that voice.

'Ah, sir. You see, sir. Dr McPherson is a doctor, sir,' James stumbled.

More 'sirs' than the House of Lords, Kirsten thought, watching the wet and distinctly aggravated man closely to see how he'd react to this blindingly obvious news.

'But still a female of the species, I presume.' More a growl than a reply. Not a good reaction.

Brown—his eyes were brown, Kirsten realised. And right now they were boring into the lieutenant as the young man floundered into a string of half-sentences, obviously trying to find an answer which would satisfy his superior while not arousing more ire in the aforementioned doctor.

She smiled encouragingly at him, amused by her reading of the situation. True, she'd snapped at him earlier. More than snapped in fact. She'd let loose the full force of the anger and frustration built up over weary months of fighting for the survival of Murrawarra's hospital.

Perhaps she should make up for her outburst by rescuing

him now. She took another step forward, invading the interloper's space.

'You might understand the situation better if you talk directly to me, rather than using James as an intermediary. If spoken slowly and carefully, I can understand English.'

The brown gaze swung towards her, the man's startled expression suggesting that he wasn't used to people addressing him without permission. Possibly written! For a moment Kirsten wondered about the penalties for insubordination. Were firing lines still used in today's army?

'I'm Major Harry Graham, in charge of this operation, and this building is to be used as the company's HQ,' he snapped, ignoring her smart comment. 'We'll be setting up our own FAP so your services won't be required. I'll give you an hour to pack, then you, and whoever else is squatting here with you, will be ferried into Vereton.'

Ken arrived right on cue. Six feet one and drop-dead gorgeous, he was also one of the best general nurses Kirsten had ever seen in action.

'Rob West phoned to say he's bringing Cathy in,' he said, ignoring the two intruders with masterly aplomb. 'He'll leave her at the water's edge downtown then he has to get back to the property. He wants someone there to meet her in an hour. Actually, it will be less than an hour now, as Chipper needed a bottle. Thirty-five minutes would be closer. He'll come in near the old meatworks.'

Kirsten checked her watch.

'I'll go,' she told him. 'You mind the shop.'

Ken nodded, then, still without acknowledging the presence of the strangers, disappeared back along the corridor that led to their 'ward'.

'I want you out of here in an hour, not meeting more people to add to your squatters' colony,' Brown Eyes told her. 'This building is to be—'

'You're repeating yourself,' Kirsten interrupted. 'You

want it for your HQ, but I want it for my h-o-s-p-i-t-a-l. Do you understand that? It's a word for a place where people come when they're in need of medical attention. And if FAP stands for first-aid post, I doubt whether your first-aiders can handle all our patients. For instance, that message was from the husband of a pregnant woman who's coming in from an outlying property. I imagine her imminent arrival means she's in labour.'

'She should have been airlifted out!' the infuriated soldier growled at Kirsten. 'Her evacuation should have been a priority. Maybe you don't understand the severity of this situation. There's a wall of water approaching this town that could destroy ninety per cent of the buildings, to say nothing of the already affected water supply and sewerage. It's no place for pregnant women.'

'Woman, singular,' Kirsten corrected him. 'And the convent has its own water supply, generators and a septic system. It's also high enough above the projected flood level to be safe. I imagine that's why you want it for your CP.'

Dark eyebrows knitted as he frowned at her.

'CP?'

'Command Post,' Kirsten responded, grinning at her feeble attempt at humour. 'Feel free to adopt it if it isn't already one of your set of initials. Now, if you'll excuse me, I've patients to see.'

'Patients? You've other patients here as well? Good heavens, woman, don't you understand the danger? Why weren't they evacuated earlier? Who authorised you staying on in the town?'

Kirsten forgot about feeble humour, as her anger, easily aroused these days, flared again.

'Now, see here, buddy!' she retorted, stepping closer to the man and stabbing her finger into his chest. 'I don't need authorisation from anyone to do my job! I am bound by an oath your rule-book mind could never understand, by things like compassion and humanity, concepts people like you ignore because you can't show them on a graph or measure their effectiveness with numbers.' She paused, then gave another stab. 'And don't call me ''woman''. Ever! Understand that? My name is McPherson, Kirsten to friends, Dr McPherson to you.'

Harry stared down at this little pipsqueak of a woman who had the temerity to be poking *his* chest. Shiny brown curls framed a face that would have been right at home in an old painting—perhaps with a blue ribbon, to match the blue of her eyes, threaded through the hair.

He was wondering where he'd seen just such an image when another sharp jab to his sternum brought his mind back to the present.

'I can't say I'm pleased to meet you, Dr McPherson,' he told her, realising he must be tired for his mind to be wandering the way it was. Now it was wondering how long it had been since he'd seen blue sky, and if it really was the same colour as those angry eyes.

He straightened his shoulders and continued. 'As I said earlier, I need this building and I don't have time to argue about it. The latest estimates are that the flood will peak here within the next three to five days—which doesn't give me and my men much time to raise the levee banks and do whatever else we can to save what's left of the town.'

The blue eyes took on a stormy look, darkening in colour as he watched.

'You took long enough to get here,' she snapped at him. 'This is the third flood to head towards us in as many months. Which is why the hospital is operating from this building. The first flood destroyed the hospital outbuildings, and weakened the foundations of the main structure so badly that the second lifted it up and took it two hundred yards downstream, then set it down out of kilter so the floor slopes every which way. That and the smell are not conducive to good patient care.'

She was sidetracking him. He knew it instinctively, although he couldn't guess why.

'You'll have to go,' he said, and saw the defiance flare in her eyes.

'We're not going,' she told him, then she stepped back and added, 'But there's plenty of room. We use the west wing of the building for the hospital, also the old dining room and some small rooms I assume were once offices. The kitchen is between the two wings—out there beyond the stairs—and big enough for us to share.'

Harry closed his eyes for a moment, hoping to relieve the tension building in his head, then said, 'We won't share because you're leaving.'

The words should have been strong and forceful but came out slightly strangled as a sneeze got caught up in them.

'Perhaps you should change out of your wet clothes,' she offered helpfully. 'I'm short-staffed at the moment and wouldn't like to have too many extra patients in the hospital.'

He was just wondering about the punishment for strangling a civilian, when she turned and whisked away, disappearing down the dim passageway her henchman had used earlier.

A shuffling sound reminded him who was to blame for all of this and he turned to Ross and demanded, 'Where's Captain Woulfe? He's supposed to have had this in hand.'

'He was detained at the council chambers, sir. Seems the mayor has a list of the properties he considers top priority. Captain Woulfe suspects he owns them, sir, and is checking the contour maps against the mayor's list.'

Harry sighed, then sneezed again. A rumbling noise outside suggested that more trucks had arrived, having travelled over the treacherous mountain track that was the only open road leading into the town. Maybe he'd get those dry clothes before long.

He nodded towards the stairs.

'Set us up in whatever rooms are available upstairs and in the east wing your doctor friend was talking about. I'd better go along on this rescue mission for the pregnant woman. We can't afford to appear anything but helpful to civilians in this situation. While they're here!'

He watched Ross take the steps two at a time, then headed down the corridor in search of the cheeky doctor. Hospital indeed! The place was over a hundred years old and probably as unsanitary as hell. He pushed open the first door on his right and was greeted by a bedridden elderly man, strung up in so many weights and pulleys he looked like something out of a comic movie.

'Morning!' the patient said. 'Young Kirsten told me the army had landed. Think you'll win the war against the water?'

'Were you offered the opportunity to be evacuated?' Harry ignored the jibe. He couldn't afford to be diverted by trivial conversation. 'I understood all hospital patients had been transferred to Vereton and the hospital closed after the second flood.'

'Ha, state government ploy, that's all that was,' the feisty gent replied. 'But they couldn't take me, could they? Not all strung up like this. One jolt of the ambulance and me pelvis would all come apart again. No, sir, they couldn't take me.'

He sounded so pleased with himself, as if being stranded in the flood-bound town were a prize of some kind, that Harry again suspected there was another agenda here, but he didn't have time to pursue it at the moment.

'Where can I find Dr McPherson?' he asked.

'Down the hall, last door on the left. It was a little sitting room originally. The nuns used it when their families visited. Kirsten's made it a combined office and bedroom as she's kind of on duty at night as well and she can hear our bells ring.'

He reached out and lifted up a small device, like a front doorbell.

'I can call her for you if you like.'

'No, I'll find her,' Harry said, preferring to argue with her without an audience this time.

He grinned to himself as he strode down the corridor. Why was he so certain there'd be an argument?

'I do not need an escort to drive down the hill and bring back one pregnant patient,' Kirsten said, when the very wet major appeared in her doorway and suggested going along with her.

'Nevertheless, you'll have one,' he said, in a placid voice she found even more irritating than his order-giving one. 'What are you driving?'

'What's that got to do with anything?' she demanded. 'It's a Toyota if you must know, and you'll make the seats all wet.'

She didn't add that she'd picked up so many wet patients in recent weeks that her car upholstery was already sprouting an interesting variety of fungal growths. She walked down the passage, pulled on her raincoat with its slick oiled coating and plunged out into the unrelenting rain.

Then stopped. The convent grounds were being transformed. Olive drab tents were rising like giant toadstools from the ground while workers in slickers of the same colour scurried through the rain like ants around a disturbed nest.

'Where did they all come from?' she asked, unable to believe the feverish activity on what had once been the gently sloping lawn of the convent.

'I've three platoons here already and more men on

standby if required. They all need to be housed, supplied and fed.'

He turned aside to address one of his men, then swung back to her.

'We're also preparing to take in evacuees if the families who've opted to remain on their properties need to be air-lifted out. FAP, mess tent, accommodation for troops, same for civilians, supplies, latrines—we move as a self-contained unit.'

Although he spoke crisply, Kirsten could detect pride in his voice, as if the army's efficiency pleased him, but it wasn't the efficiency that snagged her attention.

'All those men are wearing oilskins,' she pointed out. 'How come you're so wet?'

He grinned at her and she realised he was a very handsome man. In fact, the smile made him look almost human.

'Rainwear's designed to keep out rain not flood waters. We had a slight misadventure in a rubber ducky. Hit a submerged log.'

'You fell out of a boat? Into the flood water? I hope you haven't any open cuts or scratches. There are dead animals in that water that have come all the way from central Queensland. Fertile breeding ground for who knows what diseases. You should at least take off your clothes.'

'Right here and now?' he asked, the smile still lurking in his dark eyes.

Heat swamped her cheeks and she felt sixteen again as she realised she was blushing.

'Yes, if necessary,' she retorted. 'You'd be far better served taking care of yourself, instead of minding my business for me.'

'Ah, but I'm paid to serve the people of Australia, of whom, I presume, you are one. In fact, we could take my Land Rover,' he offered, waving a hand towards a bulky four-wheel-drive vehicle parked not far from her small blue car.

He'd switched the conversation with the neatness of a master strategist, but she was tired of arguing. Tired, full stop. For a moment she considered his offer. If they took his vehicle he would drive. But in the end she shook her head regretfully.

'No, it's too high and it would be too awkward for Cathy to climb into the seat,' she said, and led the way towards her car.

'I'll drive, you direct me,' he suggested, his long strides taking him ahead of her so that he reached the car first and had the passenger door open before she could protest.

She hesitated, instinctively reluctant, as if driving around Murrawarra with this man posed an unnamed threat.

'Look,' she said, tilting her head so she could see into the brown eyes, 'isn't the army here to help save what's left of the town? Shouldn't you be filling sandbags, or directing your troops, or yelling orders over there where things are happening? I've been ferrying people from the water's edge to the hospital since this inundation began. I can manage one more run without your help.'

'I need to assess the situation,' he said stiffly.

'You mean, check that Cathy's pregnant? That I'm telling the truth? What's it got to do with the army?'

He sighed tiredly and for a moment she felt a spurt of sympathy for him. 'It's most irregular, having civilians in need of medical care in the front line,' he muttered.

Kirsten forgot her own tiredness and chuckled.

'I know it's rough out here, but it's not exactly war,' she told him. 'And most of the civilians in these parts are very capable people. They've had to be, to survive the rigours of the bush.'

The brown eyes met hers in a kind of challenge, but all he said was, 'I understand toughness and the rigours of the bush, and if you don't stop arguing you'll be late collecting your patient.'

Disturbed by what hadn't been said, she climbed into the passenger seat and waited while he shut the door and walked around the car. It was a small courtesy, but one which pleased her. An officer *and* a gentleman? She stole another look at him as he opened the driver's side door, and felt an unfamiliar, and totally unexpected, quiver of an elemental attraction deep inside her body.

He eased himself in behind the wheel then adjusted the seat back as far as it would go.

'Just put it back where it was when you get out,' she grumbled at him, more because she was disconcerted by her reaction to his presence than with any real annoyance at him shifting it. 'I'll never reach the pedals with it right back there.'

He shot a look at her as he started the car.

'You won't be needing to worry about where the car seat is for a while. You'll be flying out of here later today. Just as soon as I can bring in some Blackhawks. The car will stay!'

'I'm not going anywhere,' she told him stubbornly. 'Not while I've patients here who need me.'

'Your patients will also be airlifted out as soon as I can get a chopper suitable for medical evacuations,' he informed her, driving slowly past the tent city his troops were erecting.

'Checking to see they've got the tent-pegs in line?' Kirsten asked nastily, sniping at him because the other conversation was veering towards a childish 'will not', 'will so' argument.

He ignored her, steering through the stone posts at the entrance to the convent grounds and turning the car towards the town.

'You're meeting your patient near the old meatworks?'

'Yes, it's—' she began, but he'd already turned left and was heading towards the old ruined building. 'How do you know where it is if you've just arrived in town?'

'We do have maps,' he said coolly. 'Which happen to have all civilian structures marked on them, including abandoned buildings and unoccupied convents.'

The penultimate word was stressed just enough to let her know that the issue of her presence in the convent hadn't been laid to rest.

Well, that was too bad. He might have maps that showed the structures in the town, but who could map the spirit of a place?

She stared out the window at the now familiar sea of brown flood water. It was moving sluggishly today, swirling in eddies around abandoned homes and the trunks of the tall gums that had so far survived. Debris clinging to the walls of the buildings showed where the previous floods had peaked and Kirsten shuddered as she imagined the next wave of water, sweeping towards them from so far up north it had already devastated half a dozen towns.

'Rob has a tinny. He'll come from that direction.'

She pointed, peering through the rain for a first glimpse of the little aluminium runabout the farmer used, in better times, for fishing,

'He'll have to travel slowly,' her chauffeur said. 'Watching out for submerged fences and floating debris.'

The windows were fogging up and Kirsten pushed open the car door as they rolled to a halt by the water's edge. The rain eased to a kind of damp mist and she heard the chug of an outboard motor above the gurgle of the moving water.

She stepped out of the car and moved towards the shelving bank where Rob would bring the little boat in to rest.

'How far have they come? Don't you realise the dangers associated with travelling across the water? There are ci-

vilian and military helicopters available for evacuations—
why didn't you call in one of them?'

'It wasn't my choice,' she reminded him. 'Besides, most
of the helicopters are working north of here, where the
flood's peaking right now. I thought their role was to rescue
people in immediate danger.'

'So you'll admit your patient's not in immediate danger?'

Kirsten spun towards him.

'What is this? Interrogation army-style? Where are the
spikes for pushing under my fingernails? Do you pack elec-
trodes when you head off on these civilian rescue missions?

'And I told you to get out of those wet clothes,' she
added crossly, as the man sneezed again.

CHAPTER TWO

HARRY stifled a second sneeze for fear the small termagant would turn on him again. He'd known the moment the name Murrawarra had been mentioned that this was going to be one of those jobs where nothing went right. What he should have done was ignore the inner voice whispering of cowardice and gone with his instincts to set up headquarters further back from the flood water. Or switched this section of the flood-stricken land to someone else.

Too late now. He bent to grab the prow of the dinghy and drag it far enough up on the bank to stabilise it. The snippy doctor had waded into the water and was steadying the woman passenger.

The man in the boat flipped his outboard up out of harm's way, and leapt ashore, dragging the back of the boat out of the swirling water. Then, with infinite care, he bent over his wife and lifted her from the seat as if she had no more weight than a child.

Harry saw the look that passed between the couple and felt a pang of envy. He wanted to help, to offer to carry the woman, but knew the man would never give up his precious burden.

The doctor had hurried ahead to her car, where she opened the back door then turned to help the farmer settle his wife on the seat.

'Take care of her, Kirstie,' the man said, his voice harsh with either the weather or emotion.

'Don't worry, Rob, we will. And we'll keep you posted. Is your phone still working or shall we call you on the CB?'

Harry stared out across the seemingly limitless stretch of

water and wondered if any phone could possibly be working.

'The phone's fine. Thank heaven for satellite technology.'

The stranger bent into the car to give his wife a final kiss, then, without a backward glance, marched back to his boat, nodded once to Harry, who held it steady for him, then dropped the propeller back into the water and reversed away.

'We don't have time to hold streamers for departing voyagers,' the irritating doctor called to him, and he turned back towards the car and found her crouched beside the woman in the back seat of the little sedan.

'You mean she's having the baby right now?' he demanded, running through the very basic training on delivering an infant he'd once received as part of a first-aid course.

'That's why she's here,' the doctor reminded him, in a tone that oozed sarcasm.

Harry wanted to argue, to remind the woman that here was where she shouldn't be—any 'she', pregnant or not, doctor or not. They were all supposed to have been evacuated…

A loud groan from the newcomer suggested that the argument could be shelved until later, and he climbed into the car and drove swiftly back to the convent.

'Stop at the side entrance and sound the horn,' the doctor ordered. 'Then, as you're here, you might as well be useful. When Ken brings out the gurney, you can help lift Cathy onto it. Try not to sneeze on her.'

Harry stifled a retort, found the side entrance to the west wing, drew the car in as close as possible, then sounded the horn. He thought he'd heard a new tightness in the doctor's voice and, as he climbed out of the little sedan

and looked in at her, her pale face confirmed a nasty suspicion that all wasn't well.

The tall man Harry had seen earlier answered the sum-
mons with a wheeled stretcher.

'Hey, Cathy!' he said cheerfully, peering into the back
seat of the car. 'You going to cut costs and have Junior out
here or do you want the full service, including a ride inside?'

'We're coming in,' the doctor Harry couldn't quite bring
himself to call Kirsten, even in his mind, replied. 'But before we move, I want you guys to work out the best way
of lifting Cathy.'

Dr McPherson—he'd call her that!

She was still squatting on the floor of the car and must
be aching with cramp, but she seemed so totally in control
Harry wondered if he'd imagined the signs of stress earlier.

'Cathy,' she continued calmly, 'I realise this position is
uncomfortable for you but for some reason a small loop of
the baby's cord has slipped down in front of its head. I'm
holding the pressure off it with my fingers and, if possible,
I want to keep my hand where it is while you're moved,
and also keep you as flat as possible so gravity isn't fighting
against us. Think you can handle that?'

Harry heard the quietly spoken words, but the lack of
emotion didn't stop his heart accelerating into panic. He
might not be an obstetrician but he understood enough
about the birth process to know the cord was the unborn
infant's lifeline.

While the two women murmured reassurances to each
other, he thrust away the fears and considered the logistics.
He could handle logistics. He was good at logistics.

'I'll get in the other door and take Cathy's head and
shoulders,' he suggested to Ken who was looking even
more worried than Harry felt. 'Then we'll ease her out in
this direction, with you taking her legs, the doctor backing

out as best she can, while I wiggle across the seat and lift from behind.'

'We can try it,' Ken said dubiously. 'Did you follow that, Cathy?'

There was a muffled assent, but Harry guessed Cathy had got beyond agreeing or disagreeing with anything, wanting nothing more than to get the whole business over and done with.

As he climbed into the car behind her and tried to slide his legs under her body so he could take her weight as they eased her out, he realised the logistics weren't nearly as good as he'd imagined.

It was a nightmare, in fact, but somehow they lifted, shoved and jostled the crying woman out of the cramped space and onto the gurney, the doctor holding her position so steadfastly Harry couldn't help but be impressed.

'Now I want you to turn on your side, Cathy. Ken, prop pillows under her hips. You…' she turned to Harry '…run inside and get more pillows—second door on the left is a store cupboard.'

The rain returned at that moment, and he was about to protest that they'd be better off getting their patient out of it when he saw the grim set of the doctor's lips and obeyed instead.

By the time he returned the gurney was under cover, and Ken now worked efficiently, raising the woman's hips on the pillows, talking soothingly all the time.

'OK, let's get inside,' the doctor said, stepping away from her patient and folding her arms across her chest so her hands were tucked under her armpits. But not before Harry saw the blue-white fingers and guessed she'd been battling a lack of circulation for some time. A tightness in her lips suggested the returning blood was hurting her but she said nothing of her own discomfort.

Harry helped Ken wheel the patient in, steadying rather than guiding as he had no idea where they'd go next.

'I made up a bed in the room next to Chipper, or the theatre's ready if you want to use it as a labour room?' Ken made the statement into a question, then turned apologetically to their patient. 'Sorry we haven't got a fancy delivery suite, Cathy,' he said. 'Like most everything else in the town, it got washed away.'

The woman smiled at him.

'As long as my baby's a Murrawarra kid I don't care if it arrives here in the corridor,' she told him, then stopped abruptly as pain again gripped her body.

'We'll go into the theatre,' the doctor decided. 'It's the mother superior's old room so that's highly appropriate. I'm sure Cathy'll be a most superior mother.'

Her tone was light but Harry could still see tension in her face and hear it beneath the words. He let Ken wheel the patient away and turned to the doctor.

'You're worried about that woman,' he said. 'Do you want her flown out?'

She looked up at him and the brown curls, lying damply against her pale skin, seemed to make a frame for her face.

'There's no need for panic,' she said tiredly. 'The baby's fine, the foetal heartbeat strong. I'd prefer Cathy deliver naturally but if I think for one moment the prolapsed cord is likely to compromise the baby's health or well-being I'll do a Caesarean.'

She frowned at him, as if distracted by some secondary thought, then added, 'This is normal hospital routine. A situation that can arise at any time. Statistically, one in four hundred births have some degree of prolapsed cord involvement. The fact that Murrawarra is all but surrounded by water is purely incidental.'

'So why are you over-explaining?' Harry demanded. 'Explaining at all? Because you shouldn't be here, that's why. And a responsible doctor would have insisted that the woman was evacuated days, if not weeks, ago.'

The doctor in question looked slightly shaken, or so he thought until he caught the flash of anger in the blue eyes.

'Insisted?' she snorted. 'Ordered, I suppose you mean! Well, I don't work that way. As far as I'm concerned, people are entitled to make their own choices and decisions. Rob and Cathy had livestock to consider—cattle and sheep Rob wouldn't have been able to shift on his own in these circumstances. Do you think she stayed behind to make life difficult for me, or to aggravate the army when it finally came swanning into town?'

She gave him a sardonic glare and continued, 'Women out here in the west share the workload with their men. They share the bad times as well as the good times, though those have been few and far between lately. But...' And now she jabbed him again with that pointy finger. 'If this couple have managed to save some stock, and the flood waters eventually recede, then at least they'll have something to build from, some animals to enjoy the good season that will follow the rains.'

She spun away from him but not before he'd heard her mutter, 'That's if we don't get a plague of locusts!'

He stood in the corridor, sneezed a couple of times and thought about what she'd said.

Was it really so tough, the life out here? So tough that a pregnant woman had put her health at risk to help her husband save stock?

And beyond that thought was another he didn't want to pursue because it was about his own choice of career—and toughness—and proving something!

A loud cry of pain brought his mind back to the labouring woman, and he felt his heart jolt with concern as if, by meeting her in these bizarre circumstances, he'd somehow become emotionally linked to her and the child she was struggling to produce.

According to the smart-mouthed doctor, Cathy wasn't at risk. This hitch in the delivery could have happened anywhere, to anyone. So why was he standing in the corridor, worrying about the woman's welfare, when he should be commanding his company?

The doctor re-emerged and he grabbed her arm.

'I can call in a helicopter,' he said urgently, and the little snip of a thing had the hide to smile at his concern.

'Women do cry out during labour,' she reminded him. 'If you can't stand the noise, get out of earshot. Go and shout at your troops. Have a parade. Get into some dry clothes.'

She whisked away and he was about to go after her, although he wasn't sure why, when a loud eruption of a different noise made him glance towards the main entrance.

As far as he could make out, there were a number of people thundering down the stairs.

People?

Very small people?

A woman bustled past him, heading towards the furore, and he followed, reaching out to take her arm and ask, 'Children?'

'Little hellions more like!' she snorted, reaching the big entry hall and yelling for quiet.

The noise level dropped but when the three children lined up in front of the woman and began, all at once, to offer excuses, it rose again.

'Silence!' Harry snapped, and this time the command worked. A scuffling noise halfway up the stairs made him look up, to see a very embarrassed lieutenant cowering in the shadows.

'Can you explain this, Ross?' he demanded, stilling the smallest child, a grubby-looking boy, with a steely glare.

'No, sir,' James replied, but he did at least descend to ground level. 'Well, they're children, sir, and they were upstairs in an attic kind of place. Seems they play there.'

'We scared him!' the eldest child, a girl, said cheekily. 'We made creaky noises on the floor and he got ever so scared.'

'And him a soldier,' the second girl scoffed.

'Then he chased us,' the little boy put in, and he stuck out his tongue at James who was hard put, Harry guessed, not to respond in the same manner. The noises he'd heard had been happy ones, if somewhat loud. Without a doubt Lt Ross had been playing with the kids.

'You know you're not supposed to make any noise downstairs,' the woman Harry had followed told the children. 'Go on through to the kitchen and you can have a bit of my mind with your morning tea.'

'Ooh, we love a bit of your mind!' the older girl cooed, teasing the woman with her smiling eyes.

'Can we have cream on it, Bella?' the younger one demanded, reaching out to take the little boy's hand.

The children capered off, milling about the woman who flapped her hands at them and scolded softly.

'Are there any more up there?' Harry asked his lieutenant.

'Not as far as I know,' the young man replied. 'But it wouldn't surprise me. The place is like a rabbit warren. And speaking of same, sir, there *are* rabbits, though only four as far as I could see. The whole top floor's set up like a playground for those kids.'

'Funny the doctor didn't mention them,' Harry mused, then he caught the gleam in his subordinate's eye and realised why the aggravating young woman had chosen not to mention children. He shrugged.

'I've had a particularly trying morning,' he said gruffly, and sneezed three times as if to prove his point.

'Are you still in those wet clothes?' a voice that was fast becoming familiar demanded. She swept into view, and bestowed a radiant smile on James. 'There's tea made and fresh scones in the kitchen, Lieutenant, if you're allowed to take a break. I'm sorry the children teased you, and I can't promise it won't happen again. They're so full of energy, and being cooped up like they are—well, it's hard for them.'

'About those children—' Harry began, but the sound of a bell ringing down the gloomy passageway had the doctor walking briskly away from them again.

'Well, tea and scones sounds good to me,' James said cheerfully. 'I had your kit put in the first room on the left as you go up the stairs, if you want to get out of those wet clothes.'

Harry stopped his roar of outrage with difficulty, contenting himself with a snarl at his junior officer and with stamping up the stairs. Until he remembered Cathy and her pain, and trod more quietly.

He changed into dry clothes, found a slicker and made his way back down the stairs and out to where the tent city was now all but complete. No one had offered him tea and scones.

'You're doing well,' Kirsten told Cathy, who was kneeling on the bed, her head down on a pillow and her hips the highest part of her body. 'And as long as you're relatively comfortable like that, I'll let the labour proceed normally.'

She had a drip running into Cathy's arm and a foetal scalp electrode monitoring the baby's heart. Now all they had to do was keep Cathy as comfortable as possible and wait.

Which gave her time to think about the army's invasion. Not a good idea!

'Ring for me if you need me,' she told Ken. 'I want to

check on our other patients, particularly Chipper, who's feeling frisky so will be looking for mischief, and old Mr Curtis. If he's up and about all the activity will have disturbed him.'

'It won't have worried Chipper,' Ken said. 'He's been spoiling for a fight since the decision to close the hospital was first mentioned. Having an officious army major around the place will give him a bit of fun.'

'He's not here to have fun,' Kirsten reminded the nurse. 'And I'd just as soon he didn't argue with the army major. That man wants us out of here, and I don't doubt he's got the power to achieve it if we push him too far.'

She left Ken with Cathy and made her way to Chipper's room. He was folding sheets of paper into sleek-winged missiles, one of which sailed over her head as she walked in.

'I want peaceful co-existence with the army boys,' she told him, catching the second missile in mid-flight and sending it shooting back towards her patient. 'And no enticing the kids to mischief or mutiny, Chipper—I mean that. So far our plan to stay open has worked well, but if we aggravate the major—'

'He'll bundle us out without a moment's hesitation?' Chipper nodded. 'He gave me the impression he was less than pleased to see us, but the young lad, his off-sider, seems OK, and I met another bloke, an underling of some kind, lost he was, and he seemed like a regular guy.'

Kirsten hid a smile.

'I don't think they're a special breed, army types,' she said. 'It's not a genetic trait.'

'No?' Chipper raised an eyebrow and sent a missile gliding towards the high ceiling.

Kirsten caught it as it dropped and fiddled with the paper. Of course, a fondness for giving orders couldn't be genetic, but the major's dark eyes, set in a face that seemed made for command—they'd come from dominant genes.

She was wondering what colour his hair might be, having only seen it darkly wet, when the subject of her cogitations caught another missile in the doorway and, holding it in one hand, peered in towards Kirsten.

'I was looking for you, Doctor.'

His tone suggested the search had been her fault.

'And now you've found me! Well done,' she responded, moved to sharpness by her errant thoughts. 'Have you met Mr Jones, better known as Chipper?'

The army of one advanced into the room and actually put out a hand to shake Chipper's.

'Harry Graham.'

The introduction was perfunctory but Kirsten gave him points for not putting his rank in front of his name—as some doctors she knew put their title.

'Graham, eh?' Chipper said. 'Common enough name, son, but well respected around these parts.'

The newcomer seemed to stiffen, but he said lightly, 'Then I shall endeavour not to bring it into disrepute.'

Kirsten wondered if she might have imagined his reaction. Particularly as he'd picked up a sheet of Chipper's paper and was folding a new design of missile.

'These don't have quite the range of the ones you've been folding, sir, but I think you'll find they'll beat yours for accuracy.'

He threw his missile, which skimmed by Kirsten's left ear before gliding to the floor.

'We'll see about that, young fellow!' Chipper said. 'A contest. Paper planes at twenty paces.'

'I'll leave you boys to play,' Kirsten said. She turned and walked towards the door, telling herself it was stupid to feel put out that the man who'd said he'd been looking for her should have been so easily diverted by Chipper's paper planes.

Cathy first—everything still progressing smoothly, Ken providing the support and encouragement the labouring woman had hoped to have from Rob.

'Actually, it's probably better having Ken,' Cathy told Kirsten during a lull in her contractions. 'If it was Rob I'd be worrying about how he was taking it all. This way I can concentrate on me.'

Kirsten left them to it, but as she walked out of the room she'd set up as a theatre the army caught up with her, in the person of Harry Graham.

'I put Chipper's challenge off until another day,' he said, falling into step beside her. 'I wanted to ask if you'd have time to show me over the place—you mentioned water and generators. I need to know exactly what's at hand. And exactly who you have in the building—what personnel we have to account for in any emergency.'

Kirsten stopped walking so she could turn and face him. His hair was a kind of sun-streaked golden brown.

Which didn't make him any less formidable a foe, she reminded herself.

'Did you get a personality transplant while you were changing clothes?' she asked. 'What happened to the ranting and raving about immediate evacuation?'

She saw his lips tighten and knew she'd gone too far—but, then, she usually did when she let her mouth have its way.

'I was not ranting and raving,' he said coldly. 'I was, naturally, startled to find a supposedly unoccupied building inhabited by the very people who should have been the first evacuated.'

'But now? You've had a change of heart? Realised it would be counter-productive to disrupt the lives of the people here any more than is necessary?' Kirsten challenged.

'Or is this little tour of inspection so you can draw up your plans to remove the lot of us? What do you favour? Force or stealth? Perhaps a silent commando raid in the early hours of the morning?'

'Lord, save me from all women!' the man called Harry Graham prayed, flinging his arms into the air before lowering them so he could run his fingers through his light-catching hair. 'Force or stealth? Good grief! We're here to help, lady, in case you haven't got the message. Here to save what can be saved of the town and salvage what's left when the waters finally subside. It's not a war—'

Whatever he'd been going to add was lost in a rattle of gunfire. Kirsten, whose nerves were already lacerated by the army's arrival, leapt in fright. Harry caught her and held her steady, his hands warm on her shoulders.

'It's a toy,' he growled. 'Those kids, I expect. I would have thought it's hardly conducive to hospital quiet, having the three of them around, but I have no doubt you've got some bizarre explanation for their presence in this place.'

Kirsten, who was thinking how…supportive his hands had felt on her shoulders, and how nice it would be to have a supportive someone in her life, nodded vaguely.

'They know they're not to make a noise down here and usually they obey that rule without question. It's probably James's fault. I bet he's been playing with them again.'

The growl that issued from Harry Graham's throat boded ill for James, but at least mentioning the young man had worked as a diversion while Kirsten pulled herself together.

'The children's father died of cancer six weeks ago,' she explained. 'Their mother is out on their property, trying to hold things together until the floods are past when she might have time to sort out her life—possibly even grieve, poor thing.'

'So you've adopted the children? That makes sense,' Harry said, trying to sound sardonic although the plight of newly fatherless children had unexpectedly tugged at his heart.

'There's no one else to take them at the moment. Elizabeth didn't want them going to strangers in another town while they're still coming to terms with their father's death.'

'Elizabeth?' Harry echoed, feeling a hollowness where the tugging had been earlier. It was a coincidence, nothing more.

'Their mother,' Kirsten told him. 'She's one of the local Grahams Chipper told you about, although she's Elizabeth Rogers now. Her father, the children's grandfather, is here as well. He has emphysema. He's a stubborn old man and wouldn't admit he needed hospitalisation, but he was too much for Elizabeth to cope with on her own, especially with the floods at the same time. We let him think he's here to keep an eye on the kids.'

He's here as well! The phrase echoed in Harry's ears as he battled a welter of emotions he had never expected to feel. They swamped his body, battered at his mind and choked his lungs. Then anger, born of fear, uncertainty and frustration, surfaced and he let it burn.

'All these people should have been moved out of town weeks ago!' He frowned ferociously at the aggravating doctor to be sure she got the message.

Not that it seemed to bother her. In fact, she smiled at him, the movement of her lips distracting him for a moment so that he missed the flash of fire in her eyes.

'So we're back to that refrain, are we?' she retorted. 'Perhaps you'd better go and change your clothes again. The "nice" has worn off that set!'

She spun away, and disappeared into the room where they'd left Cathy earlier. No doubt knowing he wouldn't want to follow her in there.

CHAPTER THREE

WHICH left Harry with two alternatives. He could make his own way through the building, opening doors and taking his chances on what or who might be behind them.

Or wait until Dr McPherson came out.

He had just decided that the first of these alternatives was too much to handle right now when the small boy appeared.

'Please, sir, James said we had to call you sir because that's your name. Could you tell me where Kirstie's gone because I have to 'pologise to her for making the noise with the gun? Bella had hidden it, you see, and when I saw it in the pantry I forgot about the noise it makes. My father gave it to me before he died. It's a great gun, sir—even James says it's good.'

Dark brown eyes peered anxiously up at him, and Harry, whose sole contact with children had been from within the anonymity of a Santa suit at the company Christmas party, found himself lost for words.

He hunkered down so his face was on a level with the boy's and looked at the child, trying not to think the thoughts that clamoured in his head.

'The doctor is busy right now but I'll tell her you apologised,' he said. 'Now, where are your sisters? Shouldn't you all be playing somewhere?'

The boy sighed.

'Upstairs!' he said gloomily. 'We're always supposed to be upstairs. Except when we come down to sit with Grandad, but we can't do that much because he tries to talk to us and that makes him cough and then we have to go

32

away. Libby says he's going to die soon but Bella says she's not to talk that way.'

The brown eyes grew luminous with tears.

'I don't much like people dying,' the little boy said huskily, then he added, as an afterthought, 'Sir.'

Harry felt his heart crack open and pain seep like red blood through his body. 'No, it's not much fun,' he agreed, 'but there's no use our getting gloomy about it. Especially not when I've got a ton of work to do. I tell you what. How about you come with me while I check on the troops? You shoot off and tell your sisters or Bella that you're coming with me, and I'll get something waterproof to stop you getting wet.'

The smile that lit up the small face was like a precious gift.

'We'll meet at the front door,' Harry added, hoping he sounded a lot more military and a lot less choked up than he felt.

He should never have come to Murrawarra!

Not that he'd had a choice. Orders were orders and his had said Murrawarra.

And although he could probably have pleaded some excuse...

He took the stairs two at a time, found a poncho in his kit and came more slowly back down the steps, to find the small boy standing in the middle of that vast foyer.

'You're looking very cross. If you've changed your mind I'll understand,' the child said gloomily, and Harry realised his thoughts were showing.

'No way,' he assured his new companion. 'I was thinking of other things, that's why I might have looked cross. Here, let's see if this will do the trick.'

He slid the poncho over the child's head, and shuffled it so the folds covered his clothes.

'Do you have a name?' he asked. 'I'm Harry, by the

way,' he added, holding out his hand. 'I'd rather my friends called me that than sir.'

The little boy solemnly shook his hand then raised the brown eyes to meet Harry's.

'I'm Anthony,' he said, 'and my sisters are Meg and Libby. Libby's the eldest, but Meg's the bossiest. Did you have sisters, sir? They're a dreadful pest most of the time but, with Mum not here, I guess it's better than not having anyone.'

He tucked his hand confidingly into Harry's and, without waiting for a reply to his question—fortunately, as far as Harry was concerned—he continued his artless prattle, pointing out architectural details of the building like the great banisters Kirstie wouldn't let him slide down, and generally filling Harry in on the trials and tribulations of the life of a small boy.

Once outside, his attention turned to the mechanical marvels arrayed before his wondering eyes. He demanded to know the horsepower of the trucks, where the exhaust came out on the amphibious vehicles and more intimate details of the army's mobilisation than Harry could provide.

'Ah, CSM,' he said, greeting his company sergeant major with relief, 'I don't suppose we'd have someone from the motor pool available to show young Anthony over our transport vehicles? He's staying in the old building and going a bit stir-crazy, being kept inside all the time.'

If Bill Jordan thought the request odd, he had the good sense not to say so.

'Can do, sir,' he responded, then he bent towards the child. 'You want to come along with me, young fella?'

Anthony looked up at Harry.

'Are you coming, sir?' he asked, apparently forgetting the order to call his new friend by his first name.

For a moment Harry almost weakened and agreed to go along, but he knew there were a string of matters demanding his attention. For a start, he had to track down Captain Woulfe and find out what was happening about the protection of the buildings in the main street.

'Sorry, Anthony, but I'll have to catch up with you later. In fact, I'll come and collect you in an hour or so and take you back to Bella for your lunch.'

He would pin Kirsten McPherson down at the same time, and insist on a tour of the building while he was over there.

Anthony nodded, accepting the compromise, and went happily off with Bill, but the thought of touring the building—and meeting the as yet unmet occupants—left Harry feeling queasy.

And reconsidering an enforced evacuation of the entire population of the old convent.

It should be easy enough to organise. All he had to do was call in aviation support and airlift the lot of them to Vereton. He'd go to his office and arrange it right now. And within a couple of hours he'd have everyone out.

He turned to head back to the building then hesitated.

Except perhaps Cathy who was probably better not being moved any more at the moment.

And old Chipper, in case his pelvis came apart again.

Welfare people would take care of the kids...

He sighed, and reversed his direction.

Kirsten checked on Cathy's progress, then, leaving orders to be called if there was any problem, she left Ken in charge while she visited her other patients. Mr Curtis first. The old man was up and dressed, sitting in a chair in the corner of his room, studying a paper he held upside down in his hands.

'Good morning,' Kirsten greeted him, and received a singularly sweet smile in response.

Realising that this particular patient was unaffected by the army's arrival, she stayed only long enough to be polite then moved on to the next room. The bed was neatly made, and the room empty. Perhaps Mr Graham had felt well enough to go upstairs and watch the children play. He could still manage the stairs on his good days, and as the small oxygen canister he could wear like a backpack was also missing she assumed he'd taken it to help him along the way.

Young Peter Phelps was next. He was one of the town's able-bodied men who had opted to stay and join the fight against the water. They were living in a scattering of houses on a hill on the opposite side of town, houses that still had the old septic systems. Knowing the worst was coming, they had planned ahead with provisions, a couple of tankers of water and a variety of communication devices in case the phones failed.

Peter was sitting up in bed, staring out the window towards the tent city.

'Watching the army set up?' Kirsten asked him.

'Wishing I was with them,' Peter told her. He turned towards her and she caught the longing in his eyes. 'I always wanted to join up, but Mum's so nervous about it. You know what she's like. You should have heard her go on about me staying on here instead of being evacuated.'

'She worries about you,' Kirsten said, putting the kindest interpretation she could on Marlene Phelps's fussing.

'Well, don't you go telling her I've been in hospital, or she'll say "I told you so" and I'll never hear the end of it.'

Kirsten promised not to say a word, but as Marlene was the town gossip, as well the town's most panicky parent, she knew it wouldn't remain a secret.

'How are you feeling?' she asked the young man, lifting the chart from the foot of his bed and checking the last notation.

'I'm much better,' Peter replied, but the hectic flush on

his cheeks gave the lie to the words. 'At least my head's not aching as much.'

Kirsten accepted that statement thankfully. When she'd admitted Peter with a high temperature, violent headache and nausea, she'd feared some form of systemic infection, perhaps from an open wound.

With the back road still open when he'd been admitted, she'd been able to send specimens of his blood, and fluid obtained from a spinal tap, to Vereton for testing. Infection and the various meningitis strains had been ruled out, and when his temperature had continued to fluctuate Kirsten had begun to wonder if it was a bite of some kind, possibly a spider bite, which had made his fever spike so badly.

Whatever had caused the problem, he was certainly on the mend.

'If I keep getting better at this rate, I'll be able to rejoin the men tomorrow,' he said, perhaps reading her relief in her face.

'Not tomorrow, but in a day or two,' she promised.

'I suppose, now the army's here, they won't really need me,' Peter added gloomily, and Kirsten wondered if perhaps the army might be more useful than it realised.

If she could get Peter a job answering phones or doing something static, he'd feel as if he was helping and at the same time he'd be out of the weather while his strength returned.

She'd have to speak to James about it. Better him than Harry Graham.

She talked to Peter for a while longer, then heard the bell ring for lunch. Not that anyone dropped what they were doing to eat, but it let the skeleton staff know that meals were ready for delivery to the patients. Once their charges were fed, the staff took turns to duck away to the kitchen and relax for a few minutes.

Kirsten walked back to the theatre and found that Mary Williams had taken over from Ken.

'Just while he eats,' Mary explained. 'Cathy's got used to having Ken with her, ordering her around.'

'Makes me feel at home,' Cathy explained. 'Rob's always telling me to do this and do that, especially when I'm on the tractor. Why he trusts me to drive the thing at all, I don't know.'

Kirsten checked the progress of the labour again, congratulated Cathy on the way she was handling the added discomfort of her awkward position, then went in search of Ken.

'Not long now,' she told him, meeting him outside the theatre.

'Half an hour till things get serious,' he said, and Kirsten didn't argue, knowing he had an uncanny knack of judging the progress of each woman's labour and was more likely to be right than she was.

She poked her head into Chipper's room to see if he'd been fed, and was hit by a pair of paper missiles this time. Harry Graham was sitting by the bed, young Anthony on his knee, and both the child and Chipper were looking guilty.

'We were aiming at the door,' Chipper said.

'Bella asked me to bring Chipper his lunch,' Anthony explained at the same time. 'Me and sir.'

Kirsten glanced at 'sir' and thought she caught a glimmer of a smile in his velvety eyes. The quiver she'd felt earlier reasserted itself, startling her with its intensity.

It's instinctual, nothing more, her head assured her body. Ignore it.

'Good lad,' she said to Anthony, 'but now you've delivered it shouldn't you slip through to the kitchen and have yours before Bella gets cross? I'll take ''sir'' on the tour of inspection he's so keen to have.'

The glimmer died in Harry Graham's eyes and Kirsten regretted her teasing. The man had looked almost friendly there for a moment—not to mention hunky!

Although the less she considered the hunkiness the better, given her unexpected physical reactions to his presence.

Harry realised he'd been well and truly hoist with his own petard. Until he'd come to terms with the pretty doctor's most recent bombshell, the last thing he wanted was a 'meet the patients' tour.

'Best go with her, lad,' Chipper advised. 'She might be small but she's mighty fierce when crossed. You should have heard her go toe to toe with our local Member of Parliament who'd been foolish enough to bring the Minister for Health out to visit us.'

Harry caught the pink flush in the 'mighty fierce' woman's cheeks and again thought of old paintings. A womanly woman, that's what she was, even in jeans, T-shirt and sneakers.

'You don't *have* to come,' she told him, apparently sensing his reluctance.

'No, no!' he muttered, lifting Anthony off his knee and scooting the child towards the door.

He stood up and crossed the room, then tried a smile in the hope he might feel better.

'Changed your clothes again?' she teased, the blue eyes sparkling as she looked up at him. They walked out into the passageway. 'Actually, I shouldn't torment you when you were kind enough to give Anthony a treat.' She hesitated for a moment, then added, 'And when I want to ask a favour.'

Harry sensed danger. Sparkling blue eyes could be a man's undoing, he warned himself.

He stopped so he could look directly at her.

'A favour?'

She lifted her slim shoulders in a casual shrug but he guessed it was all show.

'I'll introduce you to Peter first,' she explained, hesitantly at first and then rushing ahead as if she needed to get it all said as quickly as possible. 'He's a young patient, getting over a fever and not really well enough to be out doing physical work in the rain and flood waters. But the inactivity is already bugging him and as he's army-mad I wondered if you might have an inside job for him, answering phones, taking messages, counting paper-clips—anything.'

She must know those eyes are mesmerising, Harry decided as once again the persuasive power of their blueness was turned on him.

'Come and meet him,' she added, before he could explain that he didn't want a civilian messing with his paper-clips. And that wouldn't be entirely fair either, as back on the base there were any number of civilian clerical assistants.

The lad seemed reasonable enough, Harry decided after a brief visit with Peter Phelps. He'd pass the problem of finding him a job to James, but perhaps he'd find time to talk to Peter about a career in the army during the time he was here. Lads like him, who volunteered to stay behind, were what the army needed as recruits.

'This next patient is Moira Allison.' Dr McPherson interrupted his train of thought. 'She has motor neurone disease, which is degenerative and incurable, and involves muscle wasting. The hospital has been the only home she's known for the last few years so I didn't want her fragile health disrupted by an enforced evacuation.'

'But she's already been moved from the real hospital to here,' Harry argued, seeking ways to shore up his determination to get the patients and staff out of the danger zone. 'However well you might have set it up, it isn't a hospital.'

His guide squared up to him again, all five feet four or five of her.

'It *is* a hospital,' she told him. 'The building has been donated for that purpose. Once we get the insurance money from the old hospital to make a few more structural changes, this will not only be a hospital but will have hostel facilities for elderly townsfolk as well. Eventually we hope to put in a nursing home wing, too.'

She might sound definite, Harry decided, but a wariness in her eyes told him it wasn't quite as simple as she made out.

He ran the words through his head again and found the flaw.

'Wouldn't the insurance money be paid to the state government? Don't they own the hospital building?'

Kirsten McPherson's chin tilted up a notch.

'They might think they do,' she retorted, 'but, in fact, Murrawarra Hospital was built originally by a church aid society, and staffed by nurses paid by the church. Later a local board took it over and there's still a board who appoints staff and oversees the day-to-day management.'

'But it's considered a state government facility?' Harry persisted. 'Funded by the Health Department?'

'In part.' She made the concession reluctantly, then added, with grim honesty, 'To a very large extent.'

He had her where he wanted her and could have scoffed at her idea of getting insurance money, but for some reason getting the upper hand wasn't as satisfying as he'd expected it to be, and he changed the subject.

'Let's visit Moira, shall we?'

There were two women in the room they entered next, one made frail by illness, but with a faded prettiness that made Harry's guts clench with pity for her.

'Two visitors. How nice,' the second woman said.

She was small, and as wrinkled as the old apple he'd once left uneaten in the bottom of his schoolbag.

'This is Moira Allison.' The doctor introduced her patient first. 'And her friend, Peggy Riley. Peggy helps Bella in the kitchen but she's often to be found here with Moira. She claims she's got "the sight" so always knows what Moira wants to say.'

'And I do,' Peggy assured Harry. Her wrinkles deepened as she winked at him. 'Right now Moira's thinking it's about time we got some new talent in this town. She was always one who liked a handsome man!'

Moira smiled at Harry to share the gentle jest, and he realised there might be truth in Peggy's words. Moira Allison would have enjoyed the attention her beauty had brought her.

The doctor, meanwhile, was examining a lunch tray, obviously abandoned practically untouched.

'Well, we'd better move on,' she said, and Harry reached out to shake Peggy's hand then touch his fingers to Moira's fragile bones.

'I'll visit you again, if I may,' he said, and saw the answer in a slight movement of Moira's head.

'What happens with this... What did you call it—motor something disease?' He'd asked the question too abruptly, disturbed by the woman's plight.

'Motor neurone,' Kirsten told him. 'The muscle wasting and weakness can begin in any muscle but generally, and in Moira's case, it begins with the hands, shoulders and then lower limbs. We humans use a lot of muscles we're not aware of—our heart's a muscle, our stomachs need muscular contractions to digest food. The tongue—to chew and speak.'

She guessed he'd been affected by seeing Moira and wondered if this hospital tour was a good idea.

'She's at that stage now?' he asked, and she realised there wasn't much this man would miss.

'Yes.'

'But there must be something you can do,' he protested. 'Tube-feed her, give her vitamins in liquid. Something!'

She looked up at him and saw what looked like confusion in his eyes. He was trained to not accept defeat, so coming face to face with a reminder of man's mortality would be shocking.

'We're coming to it,' she agreed. 'But the prognosis for people with the disease isn't good. Moira's had longer than a lot of people have had, perhaps because of the support she's received from friends in the town—people like Peggy who volunteered to feed and bathe and sit with her. Under Health Department regulations, she shouldn't have been in hospital long term.'

Harry stared at Kirsten for a moment, apparently mulling over what she'd said, then he frowned and she leapt into speech again, anxious to defend the hospital and the town.

'But that's what towns like this are all about,' she told him. 'Community. People caring for each other. You might not understand that as the army probably has more regulations than the Health Department, but—'

He held up his hands.

'Hey! Hold it! I didn't say a thing. I'm still way back with Moira and liquid food. Are you always so quick to argue? Leaping into the fray before you've been attacked?'

Kirsten frowned at him.

'I am doing that, aren't I?' she admitted ruefully, smiling at him and enjoying the sensation of letting go of her anger. 'I guess I've been fighting for so long now that I see battles where none exist.'

She paused as suspicion reared again. Perhaps this being nice was simply a new tactic. Perhaps smiling at him was a mistake.

'But you came in fighting,' she reminded him. 'And you're probably still planning on getting rid of us right now. Strategy number four hundred and three—lull the natives into a false sense of security.'

He shook his head.

'I doubt I could lull you into such a state,' he told her, his eyes teasing her gently. 'What's been happening in this town to put everyone so on edge? Why were you fighting the Minister for Health?'

Kirsten sighed.

'It's a long story,' she said, 'and there's no time to tell it now. If you want to meet the rest of the patients, we'll have to hurry.'

Harry heard the weight of weariness in the sigh and wondered about the battles this diminutive doctor had been fighting. He found himself not wanting to add to her problems, not wanting to meet the people he'd been planning to evacuate.

'Look, you've got more than enough on your plate right now. Perhaps later? Does your day become less busy once they've all had dinner?'

She studied him for a moment as if trying to read his face, then nodded.

'Later would be better,' she admitted, then she grinned. 'After all, you'll be able to do a full head count by then. Cathy's baby should have arrived.'

He walked away, thinking about Cathy's baby—new life—and Moira Allison—so close to death—then his mind threw up an image of the doctor's face—her cheeky grin made lights like diamonds sparkle in her lovely eyes. A quickening of his pulse reminded him of the contrariness of attraction. Not that he could allow himself to be diverted by attraction. And a pretty woman like her was sure to be married—or paired off in some way.

He found himself wondering about the man and whether

he held his own in the constant battles they would surely have, then shook his head and reminded himself that he was here to work, not fraternise with the natives. Back to the tent city—that's where he'd head. Find out what was happening. Forget about Kirsten McPherson and her assorted patients.

Particularly the patient he was pleased he hadn't met.

CHAPTER FOUR

'WHERE'S Captain Woulfe?' Harry asked the clerk who was bent over charts on a table in his office.

'He's set up a post in the council chambers in the town itself, sir,' the soldier replied. 'Shall I raise him for you?'

Harry considered phoning his second in command then decided it would be better to see him.

'I'll go down.'

The soldier rushed away, presumably to find Harry's driver, who was doubtless getting away with doing as little work as possible. Harry walked through to the motor pool, where he wasn't surprised to discover his small friend once again in residence.

The grease-stained youngster was perched on a ladder, peering down into the engine of one of the big trucks that had brought in supplies. An equally greasy mechanic was explaining the workings of a fuel pump as he detached the 'expletive' thing from its moorings.

'Watch your language in front of the youngster, soldier,' Harry said, but quietly so the man knew it was more a suggestion than a reprimand. 'And don't you get in the way, Anthony,' he told the child. 'I'll come back and check on you later.'

But the scamp was down the ladder in a shot.

'I heard them call for your car, sir,' he said. 'Can I come with you, can I, sir? No one would let me go down to see the town, but I'd be safe with you, wouldn't I?'

The small hand had crept into Harry's again, its warmth, and the pressure of the little fingers, very seductive.

'I guess you can come,' he agreed, and ignored the startled look on the mechanic's face. 'But you obey orders, hear? If I tell you to stay in the car, you stay in the car.'

He strode out towards his Land Rover, nodded to his driver, then boosted Anthony up into the back seat.

'Seat belt!' he snapped, more to show his driver he wasn't going soft than to scare the kid, who nonetheless obeyed.

Having a driver made it easier to look around. A front-end loader was pushing sand into a pile behind the line of men—civilians and soldiers—who worked in pairs to fill sandbags with mechanical efficiency.

Beyond them other men stacked the bags along the levee bank, raising it against the encroaching flood.

In the main street, another knot of troops waded through the knee-deep water, steering a flat-bottomed boat. Perched in the back of this makeshift rescue craft was a very overweight woman, clutching a bird cage on her knee and loudly berating the soldiers as she was towed to safety.

Harry heard the raucous screech of a cockatoo adding its protests to those of the woman, and was feeling thankful that all he had to handle was one recalcitrant doctor when Anthony leant forward and grabbed his arm.

'That's Mrs Mathers and Whitey,' the excited child told him. 'Mrs Mathers said she'd rather be swept all the way to South Australia than leave her house again. Last time the waters came, and the sergeant took her to Vereton, someone got into her house and stole all her jewels.'

All her jewels? The thought intrigued Harry but he had no time to pursue it as his driver was pulling up behind a substantial, if flood-stained building—right behind the small Toyota he recognised as the doctor's car.

And in case he hadn't caught on, Anthony cried out, 'Kirstie's here.' He leapt from the car, running inside before Harry had time to issue a countermanding order.

Which, perhaps, was just as well as he had no doubt the child would have ignored him.

He was entering what he assumed was the rear door of the building when he heard a firmly issued, 'Out!' Anthony reversed his direction and shot back towards the door.

It was apparent that 'Kirstie' had more influence than the army where the small boy was concerned.

She was backing down the dark foyer, dragging something—someone—behind her.

'Ah, the major!' she said calmly. 'Good. Your man's hurt his leg. I want to get him out of here. If you take his shoulders I think I can lift his legs.'

'We need a stretcher. I'll contact our—'

'Now, Major!'

She cut across his protest and at the same time he heard an ominous creak and realised that the passage ahead of them ended abruptly. Part of the building had already collapsed.

He bent, seized Woulfe's shoulders and proceeded to drag him towards the door, hauling the injured man unceremoniously out into the rain before asking his driver to summon the FAP ambulance.

'What happened?' he asked Kirsten, who was ignoring the patient and peering into the building with a worried frown creasing the pale, smooth skin of her forehead.

A low rumble and a cloud of dust billowing out suggested there'd been more movement.

'The ceiling's collapsed. From the back the building looks OK, but just beyond where you found us the ceiling is down on floor level and heaven only knows where the floor is. Your man was in there. He crawled out—but I think Jim Thompson, our mayor, is probably trapped. And I don't know who else might have been inside.'

She stepped forward as if to go back into the building but Harry grabbed her arm and hauled her back.

'We'll stabilise it first. Did Captain Woulfe say anything? How did you come to be here?'

'Jim—the mayor—phoned. About something else. While we were speaking there was a dreadful grinding noise and we were cut off. I came straight down and found the soldier—a captain, is he? Anyway, he was lying in the passage. I should go back in. I'm small, and can probably get through wherever he came out.'

'You'll do no such thing!' Harry snapped at her, the thought of the woman putting herself in such danger making his blood run cold. 'Your job's to treat the injured. See to that lad. Get him up to the hospital and fix his leg. Driver, I want all available men down here, with hydraulic lifting gear and any props, jacks or solid timber that can be used to shore up a collapsing building.'

'There's a hardware store across the main street. I know Jack Henry wired his timber into packs in the hope it wouldn't float away,' Kirsten told him, looking up from where she crouched beside her patient.

Harry nodded acknowledgment of her suggestion and was about to walk away to inspect the building from the outside when the company's ambulance, apparently alerted by his driver, pulled up and two orderlies jumped out.

'We need a stretcher,' Kirsten told them, then she straightened and turned to Harry.

'I'll take him to the hospital, X-ray him and set his leg. If there are any complications I promise you I'll arrange to fly him out.'

He was about to protest that his own men could handle the patient when she added, 'I'll take the ambulance driver and then send him back down here as soon as possible. I think you'll need all the help you can get.'

Which he would, Harry realised, if there were living people beneath the slabs of concrete inside the building.

He nodded to her and watched as she herded a protesting

Anthony into the front of the converted Land Rover, then climbed in the back to squat beside her patient.

She was having an uncomfortable day, one way or another.

Kirsten turned her attention to her new patient. He was stirring and she guessed he'd held himself together as he'd crawled out of the collapsed section of the building then had passed out from pain and exhaustion.

'The wall came down on my leg,' the man said. 'It hurts.'

'So it should,' Kirsten told him. 'It's broken. What about your head? You were out cold in there. Was your head injured?'

She leaned over him and ran her fingers over his scalp as she asked the question, seeking any lump or a softness in his skull that would suggest a depressed fracture. She checked his pupils—normal—and found no seepage of clear cerebrospinal fluid from either ear or his nose.

'I might have bumped it on the floor when I went backwards, but I can't feel any pain in it. I was at the desk—it collapsed on to my leg, but held the rest of the wall off me.'

He spoke slowly, as if trying to piece together his recollection of the moment, then he seized Kirsten's hand and tried to lever himself into a sitting position.

'There were two other men in there. Are they out? Does anyone know? They were behind me, near some filing cabinets. I didn't see them later.'

'Your colleagues are tending to them now,' Kirsten told him, knowing there was no point in getting the man more agitated. His pulse was steady and his breathing seemed unimpaired, but agitation didn't always show in physical ways. 'I'm going to get you fixed up then go back down there myself, so they'll be well looked after.'

She mentally crossed her fingers, hoping she was right

and that the two men—Jim and whoever it was?—were safe!

Anthony was directing the ambulance driver to the side entrance to the hospital.

'I'll need a hand to get him inside then we can handle things from there,' she told the driver. 'Could you tell the major there are two men still inside the building?'

He nodded, and she knew he'd be heading straight back down to the accident site.

'Anthony, you shoot inside as soon as we stop and ask Mary to turn on the X-ray machine. Then find your sisters and check they've fed the rabbits.' She knew the only way to keep him out from underfoot was by giving him a task.

Though what he'd been doing down in the town she had no idea. Probably stowed away in one of the army vehicles.

They pulled up and the child shot off as ordered. The driver opened the back of the vehicle and undid the brakes on the gurney before sliding it out, steadying it as first one and then the second pair of long, wheeled legs dropped to the ground.

Mary Williams came running out and took one end, and Kirsten assured the driver they'd manage now and waved him on his way.

'The council building's collapsed,' she said to Mary. 'This fellow crawled out but Jim and someone else are still inside.'

'The council building? It's solid stone. I can't believe that going.'

I can't believe any of this, Kirsten thought, but most of her attention was on her patient. Together they wheeled him through to the X-ray room.

'I'm going to start fluid and some painkiller running into you,' she told her patient, 'then we'll X-ray your leg and give you a light anaesthetic while I realign the bone, X-ray it again to see I've got it right, then immobilise it with plaster. Thirty minutes, and you'll be resting, more or less comfortably, in a bed.'

'Can you manage here?' Kirsten asked Mary when the patient had been hooked up to a drip. 'I want to check on Cathy and set up for the plaster.'

Mary nodded and Kirsten left her to it, heading for the theatre and worrying about the soldier as she walked.

She'd felt the grating of the bone which had told her whatever had fallen on his leg had fractured his tibia and, no doubt, fibula as well. Because the fibula wasn't weight bearing, it could be disregarded, but the tibia would need to be set and immobilised while the bone knitted together.

Should she send him on? Have him airlifted out?

She thought of the number of fractures she'd handled since arriving in Murrawarra. Where men rode motorbikes around their properties, these injuries were common. In fact, she probably had more experience than either of the doctors in Vereton who would, no doubt, send their patients to an orthopedic specialist in Dubbo.

'I'll set it,' she muttered as she entered the theatre and found Cathy and Ken both occupied in the final stages of delivery of the new addition to the West family. Merryll Cooper, the nurse's aide who'd stayed on with the skeleton staff, was hovering over a trolley set up with a baby bundle containing everything that was needed to welcome the new arrival to the world.

'You sneaked up on me,' Kirstie said to Cathy, who was pushing and panting and cursing the absent Rob all at once.

Ken had looped the problematic cord well out of the way so the head slid past it without risk of strangulation. As Kirsten watched, Ken gave a competent twist, the shoulders came through and a tiny baby boy slid out and was held aloft for his mother to admire. Then, when he gave his first cry of protest, he was handed to her.

'Well done, all of you,' Kirstie said. She glanced at Ken. 'You can manage?'

He nodded and she knew she hadn't had to ask. He loved maternity work, and fussed more than the mothers over the babies in his care.

'Don't forget to phone Rob,' she reminded Cathy. 'As soon as you're both cleaned up, Ken will settle you into bed and bring you a phone.'

She left the beaming mother and went towards the room they'd set up, more than slightly tongue in cheek, as the plaster room.

It had been a small chapel, now deconsecrated but still adorned by plaster saints who seemed to watch approvingly over the work. She pulled out what she'd need, at the same time preparing herself mentally for the task ahead—first aligning the bone, then stabilising and immobilising it. She'd need Mary's help.

Again doubt surfaced. Should she send him on?

Lt Ross appeared as she was debating this.

'The major said to tell you we're on our own for at least three hours. The Vereton police have just advised the back road's now cut, and our choppers are grounded behind the floods until new fuel's flown in. Apparently it will take that long to bring back one of the search and rescue choppers from the action further north.'

The bit about the fuel made absolutely no sense at all to Kirsten but she understood that the major was actually giving her permission to set his soldier's leg.

Though the other men, if badly injured…

'Has he asked for a civilian chopper?'

'He's told them what's happened and warned them one might be needed,' James replied.

Kirsten nodded, hoping in her heart that one would be needed. The alternative was too grim to consider. And the flood peak hadn't reached them yet.

Returning to the X-ray room, she found her patient all but asleep, the soporific effect of the drugs already working. Mary had the films up in light-boxes, and Kirsten studied them. The break in the tibia was clear but clean, and there were no dark shadows to suggest blood-vessel involvement.

When she reduced the fracture in the tibia, the fibula would also move into alignment. A simple task, she assured herself, annoyed that the major's sudden appearance in her life should be making her doubt her professional ability.

With her patient temporarily knocked out by a mild anaesthetic, Kirsten moved the lower limb until she was satisfied the bone was realigned, then manoeuvred the gurney back for another X-ray.

'Spot on,' Mary told her, holding the film up to the light before slotting it into the box.

Kirsten studied it closely, then nodded her agreement. Now all she had to do was plaster the limb.

All? It was a dreadful job, one she was sorry she hadn't left to the army first-aid personnel who doubtless could set limbs.

With Mary's help she wheeled their patient to the plaster room. She had a treasured supply of one of the new synthetic cast materials, thermoplastic strips that dried in thirty minutes. It was lightweight, easy to wear and impervious to water, so a patient could shower, or even swim in it, although she wouldn't recommend that the captain do any swimming for a while.

'Will you use the expensive material?' Mary asked, guessing at her thoughts.

'I think so,' Kirsten replied. 'The army deserves the best. My only doubt is my own ability. It's more difficult to apply.'

'Only because you have to work more quickly,' Mary pointed out. 'And you're neat and speedy with your hands when you're applying plaster.'

Buoyed by the nurse's confidence, Kirsten made her decision.

The soldier raised sleepy eyelids and Kirsten told him what she was about to do, then watched him drift back to sleep.

While Mary filled a bowl with water and slid plastic sheets and a small foam prop under the patient's leg, Kirsten prepared thin, pliable splints to incorporate into the plaster. Later a heel support would be added, but that would depend on when X-rays suggested he could safely bear weight on the injured leg. She eased a length of stockinette up onto his thigh where the top edge of the plaster could rub, put padding around his knee to protect the bony protuberances, put another stocking over his ankle and heel, and more padding around the bone.

'The main thing is to work with the palms of the hands,' she told Mary as she took the wet strips of material from the nurse and moulded them around the patient's leg. 'Using the fingers can leave indentations that press on the patient's skin.'

'It's a knack I tried to master when I first began nursing,' Mary said, 'but I never got the hang of it. My palms don't work like my fingers do. I'm glad there's always been someone else around who was better at it than I was.'

'You mightn't be the best plasterer in the world, but you'll do me as an assistant,' Kirsten told her. 'So many people can only do one thing at a time—like wetting the material. You're feeling the patient's skin, checking its integrity and gauging the temperature at the same time. I can explain a hundred times to some nurses about the chemical reaction between the impregnated cloth and water causing heat, and they still wouldn't feel it as I work.'

Mary grinned at her. 'Hey, there's no need to butter me up. I offered to stay, remember?'

Kirsten looked up from her task to meet Mary's eyes. 'We did do the right thing, staying? Didn't we?'

Mary's smile faded. 'That army major giving you a hard time?'

Kirsten shrugged and Mary continued. 'Of course we did the right thing. In fact, you agreeing to stay on saved a lot more trouble than that officious gent realises. It was only when you said you were staying, no matter what happened, that most of the locals agreed to go. Otherwise they'd all have camped out on the hill here, if only to save the hospital.'

Kirsten smoothed the last strip into place then ran her palms down over the plaster to make sure it was snug enough to immobilise the bone.

'Will you clean him up? And trim the ends of the cast as soon as it's set. I'll send Ken in to help you get him into bed. Leave the cast uncovered and test his toes for neurovascular compromise every hour. Talk to him at the same time, make him respond. I want to know if there's the slightest indication of delayed concussion. I'm going back down to the council chambers but I'll have the cellphone if you need me.'

Mary raised her eyebrows but knew better than to argue, and Kirsten hurried away, wondering if an hour had been long enough for the soldiers to have stabilised the building.

And if anyone else could possibly have survived the collapse.

She found James hovering in the corridor, and asked him to drive her back down to town. It was only a kilometre, but arriving dry would be nice.

'I'm in charge up here,' he replied, but his tone told her what he thought of such a tame position.

'You needn't be away long and I promise you no one will steal the building or go through your top secret files.'

He blushed and smiled and dipped his head.

'Wait at the side door while I get transport,' he said. 'And if the major tears strips off my hide I'll blame you.'

By the time Kirsten had told Ken her plans and asked him to give Mary a hand, James was waiting outside with yet another version of an army-modified Land Rover.

'This one's a mobile office. In fact, Major Graham usually drives it. Though when he went down town earlier he wouldn't have realised he'd be staying there.'

Kirsten climbed in. The rain had settled into drizzle, suffocatingly wet, turning the day a uniform and depressing grey. The scene at the council chambers was brighter, generator-powered arc lights beaming into the building, men throwing roof tiles aside as they dug down from the top.

James, perhaps correctly interpreting a look from his superior, suggested he leave Kirsten and return to the convent, and she thanked him for the lift and got out.

'I assume you're down here to collect your car,' the major greeted her, stepping forward as if to block her way if she dared go near the building.

'You might need help when you reach those two men,' Kirsten told him.

'I have help,' he said curtly. 'How's Woulfe?'

'I've set his leg. He's resting.'

She didn't add the usual 'comfortably' as she was reasonably certain the captain was anything but comfortable. And she made sure her words were every bit as curt as Harry Graham's had been.

'Have you had any contact with the men, any signals they might be alive?'

He shook his head and the bleak look in his eyes made Kirsten feel almost sorry for him.

'The floor was concrete, and the walls and ceiling that collapsed in are solid plaster. I don't know that we'd hear someone knocking.'

Kirsten nodded. 'It was a solid old building,' she agreed. 'Which makes its collapse even harder to understand.'

'I think the previous floods have been scouring away underneath it. Perhaps a new watercourse formed and, with this next inundation coming down, more earth was washed away—undermining the foundations at the front corner and causing the collapse. It's imploded inward, not gone outward.'

'Like a house of cards,' Kirsten muttered, remembering the rainy-day occupation of her childhood and her frustration when a delicately balanced structure collapsed.

'We've got props in place internally, sir, and men working from the top down, but it will take hours to get through that way because we're not sure where to concentrate.'

The young soldier who made the report nodded to Kirsten, but it was no more than automatic politeness. The major had all his attention.

'Can you reach the trapped men?' Harry demanded, and Kirsten watched the man shake his head.

'Private Forde tried, sir. He's our smallest man, but even he can't get a jack in far enough to enlarge the hole. The men are working on it—digging at it by hand, not wanting to use too much force in case it collapses altogether. As it is, he says he saw light and what appears to be a bigger space beyond the passageway.'

'What good would it do, getting the jack further in?' Kirsten asked, knowing any further delay could mean the difference between life or death for the two trapped men.

'We could attach a hose to the jack, and use air pressure to raise the collapsed wall enough to get help to the men.'

'I'll take the jack in,' Kirsten told him. 'Once I've set it up, I might be able to get right through.'

'I won't allow it!' the major snapped.

'You've no alternative!' Kirsten snapped right back. 'I'm the smallest person here, and I'm also the best equipped to provide help to the trapped men. Just give me a minute to get some gear from my bag.'

She hurried away before he could argue, found her bag and extracted what she might need, tucking the drugs and bandages into pockets then making up a sealed plastic bag of secondary requirements which the army could send through to her later if she needed them.

'If I tie a bit of that to my waist,' she told the major, pointing to some of the fine rope coiled on the ground, 'I can let you know what else I need—this bag of stuff, the small oxygen tank, whatever. You can tie it on and I can pull it through.'

The brown eyes were bemused, then they darkened—she guessed, with anger.

'You're not going in there,' he said, and Kirsten sighed.

'Let's not do this,' she pleaded. 'We're wasting time. You have the place propped. It's quite safe and someone has to go. Give me this jack, tell me what you want done and let's get on with it.'

He hesitated, then looked around, finally nodding abruptly, although Kirsten knew from the grim set of his lips that he was far from happy about it.

Rather than push him further, she crossed to the rope, but he strode ahead and bent down, lifting the coil and hefting it in his hand before turning to a soldier with a curt order.

Another man appeared with a harness and a coil of what looked like bright orange twine.

'This is strong, but lighter,' the major said to her, stepping towards her and fitting the harness over her shoulders, snapping it shut in front then fixing the twine to a loop at the back.

His closeness unnerved her, so she stuttered when she said, 'A-afraid my knots will c-come undone?'

'Afraid this whole mad scheme will come undone,' he

growled, his lips so close to her ear she could almost feel them move. The quiver returned but she put it down to apprehension of what lay ahead of her.

He stepped back and looked down into her eyes.

'We've pushed metal props like long thin triangles along the corridor. They should hold, but if you hear any noise, any creaking, get out of there.'

Kirsten nodded, and hoped she looked braver than she felt.

'And don't attempt to reach the room. Position the jack just beyond the props, then back straight out again. We'll enlarge the crawl space and prop it as we go. Once it's safe you can do your rescue thing.'

Kirsten glared at him. Instinct told her the trapped men would need help and the delay in getting to them was intolerable. But if she went in and brought the shattered building down on top of the three of them…

'I'll come back,' she agreed reluctantly, and was surprised when he grinned at her.

'You bet you will, Dr McPherson. I'll be holding your lead!'

He tugged at the orange rope and Kirsten felt it jerk her harness, then he put his hand on her back and guided her into the building.

'Hard hat,' he said, and slapped a miner's helmet, complete with light, on her head. 'You should be able to see but the light might pick out something you'd otherwise miss. Now, in and out—understand?'

Kirsten nodded. The space looked far smaller than it had earlier when she'd found the captain. And the 'props' seemed far too flimsy.

She took a deep breath, grasped the jack a soldier handed her and crawled into the tunnel. It wasn't too bad until crawling became impossible and she had to lie on her stomach, pushing the jack, with its air hose attached, along in front of her and squiggling inch by inch through the debris.

It was dark now and she was glad of the little lamp, glad it picked out the metal frames that ran along each side of her. Ahead, perhaps about ten feet but impossible to reach, was the lessening of the darkness which suggested open space and gave her hope.

'Jim, can you hear me? Are you guys all right in there?'

No answer, no knocking—only silence and darkness.

Hope wavered.

'Set the jack in position and get out,' the major called to her, and Kirsten, who'd considered disobeying, realised she couldn't physically go any further.

She opened the arms on the top of the jack then set it upright, wiggling it to make sure it was stable. She checked that the hose was still attached to the fitting and the connection was tight, then she began to worm her way backwards, pleased to find a steady pressure on her harness which made this easier, though to have her heels seized and be unceremoniously hauled out the final few feet wasn't what she'd have chosen.

'Come outside while they lift and prop some more.' Harry helped her to her feet and hustled her out before she could argue. 'The men will only raise it an inch at a time, pushing the props forward at the same time. Could you see how much further the tunnel stretches? Were you nearly to the end of it?'

Kirsten was about to explain when her knees began to tremble and she'd have slumped to the ground if he hadn't caught her.

'Reaction!' she said shakily. 'Boy! I've never believed that really happened. Talk about adrenalin depletion.'

Then, realising she was being held in the major's arms and his brown eyes were looking worriedly into hers, she stiffened and said, 'I'm OK now. You can put me down. I won't keel over.'

He lowered her back to her feet, but continued to hold her until a shout from his men diverted his attention back to the rescue mission.

'Sit!' he said, pointing to the passenger seat of the army vehicle behind them.

'Do I bark or salute?' Kirsten asked, but she sat anyway, pleased to get some neutral support under her, though why she should feel more shaken by the major holding her than she'd been by her crawl in the tunnel she'd consider later.

CHAPTER FIVE

IT WAS another hour before the narrow corridor into the room where the men were trapped was propped securely. Kirsten, who'd recovered her equilibrium, heard the sounds of success and got out of the vehicle, hurrying back to the building.

Several civilians had joined the soldiers, including a man Kirsten recognised as the town engineer. One name she could cross off the list of possible victims trapped inside.

'I'll go in,' she offered, meeting a dusty-looking Harry at the entrance to the narrowed tunnel.

He looked doubtfully at her.

'Are you sure you're all right?' he demanded. 'I wouldn't consider it, but my qualified men are too big to get through.'

She had to smile at his reluctance to allow her to put herself in even minimal danger.

'I'll be safe with the props in place,' she assured him.

'I'll rope you up again, and give you a walkie-talkie so we can communicate.'

Kirsten felt her smile fade from her lips. So she could tell him the bad news—that was another interpretation which could be put on his words. The silence from the two missing men wasn't a good sign.

She stood still while he fitted the vest and attached her to the orange twine. He demonstrated how to work the walkie-talkie and tucked it into a pocket of the vest.

'Now, this,' he said, handing her a thin metal pointer, 'is an aluminium probe. It's telescopic and will stretch out to about four metres so you can test your footing before you move.'

He buttoned the probe into another pocket then fitted the miner's helmet on her head and did up the strap beneath her chin.

He was so close she could see the dark shadow of his beard beneath the tanned skin on his chin. His eyes were intent on his task and he was oblivious to her tremor of reaction as his fingers brushed her overly receptive skin.

'Don't do anything foolish!' he growled, holding her captive in front of him with one hand clamped to the top of the helmet. 'If the space beyond the tunnel looks at all unsafe, get straight out of there. Don't even venture into it if you think there's an element of risk. We're still lifting stuff from the top and eventually we'll get down to where the men are.'

She nodded, because it was difficult to speak. It must be nerves making her chest so tight, her skin so prickly.

He looked at her for a moment longer, as if there was something else he meant to say, then he, too, nodded and he released her. She turned away, knelt down and first crawled, then wriggled along the now familiar tunnel.

The jack had done its work, raising the roof enough for longer props to be slid into place. Ahead was the less dense darkness she'd seen earlier—the room from which Captain Woulfe had crawled.

The floor dropped away from beneath her searching hands and she realised she'd reached the end. She turned her head so the light would illuminate the room, and saw the wall that had fallen on the soldier, the solid slab of it resting at a crazy angle against the old oak desk Jim had deemed suitable mayoral furniture.

'Jim, can you hear me? Can anyone hear me?'

She called in vain, then sniffed the air, but it was too dusty to detect the odour of blood.

Next she shined the light upwards, where she could see roof tiles. The ceiling had certainly come down in this room, perhaps burying the missing men.

Hauling out the walkie-talkie, she reported what she could see.

'I can slide out of the tunnel into what's left of the room,' she told whoever was listening at the other end. 'There's no immediate danger where I'll land—no beams directly above me, only light timber and the roof tiles.'

She peered upward again and saw a gap in the tiles.

'Once I'm in, I can poke the probe up through the tiles. If you can lift off the ones around that spot you could drop men from your crane into the room.'

She heard Harry say, 'Well done.' Then a lower-pitched warning. 'But don't do anything stupid!'

Stupider than pitching head first into this room? From the position she was in, prone on the floor above it, there was no alternative. She prayed the floor would hold and wriggled further forward, but in the end there was nothing for it but to let her body drop.

Her light went out as her helmet hit the ground, but when she reached up and fumbled for the switch she was relieved to find it was still working. The dirt and dust, not to mention the spiders, told her she was on top of what had been the ceiling. She edged closer to the wall, hoping Jim and the mystery second man weren't somewhere under her feet.

Directly above her was the hole in the tiles, which explained the light in the room.

'I'm raising the probe now,' she dutifully reported. 'Could someone yell when they've spotted it?'

She pulled out the slim metal tube and tugged until it was fully extended. She held it up and manoeuvred it until she had the point outside the hole.

A shout greeted her efforts and she let her arms drop, grateful to have the strain off them.

'I'm going to cross to the middle of the room where the desk is,' she said into the walkie-talkie. 'Captain Woulfe was sitting there, and as the wall is held up by the desk the men may be trapped beneath it.'

Stepping carefully over broken timber and assorted debris, which suggested that cartons of papers may have been stored in the space between the roof and the ceiling, she reached the desk. She knelt beneath it to shine her light into the angled space under the collapsed wall. No sign of the missing men—or, now she came to think of it, of the filing cabinets Captain Woulfe had mentioned.

'Can you hear me?'

Harry's voice came through the walkie-talkie.

'Yes, go ahead,' she answered, pressing the button back to receive.

'We're about to lift the tiles around the hole. Make sure you're nowhere near that area. In fact, get as far away as possible in case something falls.'

She told him she was by the desk, and protected by it and the fallen wall, then looked up to see a soldier dangling from the jib of the crane. Not any soldier, she realised as the hole grew bigger, but the boss.

'Isn't there a regulation in the army about officers not taking foolhardy risks?' she asked, when he was eventually lowered into the room and joined her by the desk.

He grinned at her.

'I found it quite exhilarating and, although it's not a regulation, the general rule is you don't ask the men to do something you wouldn't do yourself!'

Then he sobered and looked around. 'What a mess. No sign of the men?'

Kirsten shook her head.

'They could be under that ceiling,' she said doubtfully, 'but Jim Thompson was a big man and it looks to me as if it's lying very flat on the floor. Your man said they were by the filing cabinets which were in that corner.' She waved her hand to indicate the corner of the room, where the ceiling and part of the wall were lying at floor level.

'What's underneath? A cellar?'

Kirsten shrugged.

'I've no idea. The shire engineer was outside. Wouldn't he have mentioned a cellar if there was one?'

Harry unclipped his own walkie-talkie and asked the question, suggesting that someone ask the engineer.

'No cellar that I know of,' a man's voice told him, 'although quite often civic buildings were built on the site of previous ones. The present structure was erected in 1934, maybe on the site of an older town hall. There could have been a cellar under that.'

Harry signed off and sighed. He looked at Kirsten and frowned.

'I don't want people tunnelling in underneath in case more of the structure collapses. And I don't want too much weight in here in case there is a cellar and our men are alive in it. Let's take off your trailing rope and I'll get you lifted out, then one of the men can take your place and we'll lift the wall and ceiling. See what's what.'

Kirsten looked around. He was right—there was nothing she could do that a fit young soldier couldn't do better.

'I'll stay on site, though,' she told Harry. 'When you do find the men, they could need help.'

He nodded, and she guessed he realised that the longer it took to get to them, the less chance there was of finding them alive.

She stood as still as possible as he unhitched the rope then unbuckled the harness, not wanting to initiate a brush of his fingers against her skin when his closeness and his impersonal movements were already intensifying the strange shivers through her body.

'There,' he said when he was done. He spoke into his

radio again and the hook on the crane dropped slowly through the hole.

'You stand on here and hold onto the steel rope. Can you do that?'

Kirsten looked at the 'here', a heavy curve of metal, then down at her damp sandshoes.

'I guess so,' she told him, trying not to think about the hook rising in the air, with her dangling like a fish from a line.

'Perhaps we should do it this way,' Harry said, and he took her arm and led her towards the rope. 'I'll stand on the hook and you stand on me. I'll hold you—I won't let you fall.'

He put one foot on the hook, and swung her around so she was facing him.

'Step up on my foot,' he said. 'Come on. There's nothing of you, you won't even bruise it. Good. Now put your weight against me, and your arms around me and hang on.'

She had no choice, especially once his free hand dragged her hard against his body, an arm as taut as the steel rope holding her there. Her face was pressed against his chest, her nose buried in the camouflage fatigues, and as they swung up and out, across the ruined building, she felt his warmth and strength seducing her body into thinking how comforting it was.

He's holding you so you don't panic and fall off the stupid hook! she reminded herself as they were lowered back to earth to the accompaniment of a chorus of catcalls from the onlookers.

'Way to go, Doc!' one of the locals called to her.

'Flying high!' another wit offered, but the noise died down when the rescuers realised the two missing men hadn't been found. While Harry deployed his troops, and sent the locals back to filling sandbags, Kirsten crossed to her car and opened the front door, slumping into the driver's seat as reaction once again took the strength from her knees.

She was sitting there, debating whether to drive back up to the hospital or wait here, when Meg and Libby came racing down the hill, Anthony trailing behind.

'It's Grandad,' Libby told her. 'We've searched and searched. He's nowhere in the convent.'

Kirsten felt the coldness of certain knowledge ice her blood.

'He'll be OK,' she assured the frightened children. 'He probably felt well enough to go for a walk. You know how he feels about this town. He's been coming up with ideas of how to save it the whole time he's been at the hospital.'

Three small heads nodded their agreement, while three sets of dark eyes looked solemnly at her, waiting for her to tell them more.

She realised all three were wet, raincoats forgotten in their anxiety to find their grandfather.

'Hop in the car, I'll drive you back. Bella can make some hot chocolate while you get into dry clothes, and you can all stay in the kitchen with her—near the phone—so as soon as I track down Grandpa, you'll know.'

'Should we ring Mum and tell her?' Meg asked.

Kirsten shook her head, more to rid herself of the thought of more pain for Elizabeth than in answer to the child's question.

'No. It would only worry her and he's probably safe and sound somewhere. But if he's down there filling sandbags in the wet, I'll give him what for!' she added sternly, and the children all laughed.

She drove them back to the old convent, hustled them upstairs and went through to the kitchen.

'I'm sorry, Bella, but I've promised them hot chocolate and then suggested they stay in here with you.'

In an undertone she shared her fear that the second man

missing at the council chambers was the children's grand-father.

'Oh, the poor lambs. As if they haven't been through enough already. I'll keep them by me. We can make gingerbread men. I might have some hundreds and thousands—we could make gingerbread houses as well.'

She patted Kirsten on the arm.

'Now, don't you fret about the kids. You have more than enough on your plate. You could probably do with a hot drink yourself before you go back down there. You look like something the cat dragged in.'

Kirsten gave wry thanks and looked down at the dust embedded in her jeans.

'I guess there's no point putting clean clothes on.' She sighed. 'As soon as I do I'll have to crawl through a small space again. Speaking of which, I won't stop for a drink.'

She gave Bella a quick hug.

'The sooner we get to the men, the more chance there is of finding either or both of them alive.'

She looked in on Captain Woulfe, and was pleased to see he was feeling well enough to be flirting with Mary, then she found Ken and explained what was happening, leaving him in charge while she headed back to the town.

'We've lifted the ceiling and the collapsed wall,' Harry told her when she returned to the scene where men worked with careful efficiency. 'And we've been propping the lower level of the building from the outside in case we have to tunnel. The floor in that room seems relatively intact, apart from a hole in one corner. There's a chance they went through in that area but nothing much followed them.'

'So they could be sitting snugly down there in the cellar, waiting for us to come?' Kirsten asked, disbelief colouring her words. 'Why haven't they called out? Why haven't we heard them?

Harry's brown eyes looked down into hers and she

sensed his impatience with her questions, but before he could answer her a shout from one of his men had him striding away from her.

She followed, almost trotting to keep up with him.

'I think I know who the second man is,' she told his soldier-straight rear view. 'I think it's Mr Graham—the children's grandfather. He's not up at the hospital and it makes sense that if he was feeling well enough to want to help, he'd have come to the council chambers. He was shire president for more than thirty years.'

Harry stopped abruptly and she slammed slap bang into the straight back, losing her balance and tilting dangerously to the side before he swung around and his hands once again caught and stabilised her.

'Why would a sick old man put himself into danger like that?' he demanded, and Kirsten, who'd thought he'd be pleased to have the second man identified, stared at him in total mystification.

'Because he's that kind of man,' she said lamely. 'Although all the town has been involved in the fight to save the hospital, he's the one who bought the convent and donated it for that purpose. Murrawarra is his home, *his* town. Of course he'd try to save it.'

'And die trying?' Harry asked savagely, then he turned and strode away again. Only this time Kirsten didn't follow.

He could darned well call her if he wanted her.

She picked up her bag and walked across to the military ambulance to check out its fittings, something she'd not had time to do while riding in it. It had all the standard equipment, including emergency resuscitation gear.

'Like what you see?'

One of the orderlies she'd met earlier came around to the back.

'It's fantastic,' she said. 'So compact. I'm glad you're here. Our ambulance was seconded to duty in Vereton—

the theory being that the ambulance should be where the people were.'

'Typical bureaucratic thinking,' the man replied. 'At least in the army, the men come first.'

Anything else he might have been about to say was drowned out by the beat of helicopter rotors. One of the small government search and rescue helicopters was circling overhead.

'Have we radio contact with that chopper?'

The major's voice cut through the escalating noise.

'I've got the pilot on line,' a man called back.

'Then tell him to get the hell out of here. He can land up near the old convent somewhere, but not so close to our tents that his downward thrust will blow them to bits.'

Kirsten held her breath until the helicopter lifted back into the air and swung away.

'Bloody cowboys!' she heard Harry mutter, and her heart quailed as she realised why he'd panicked.

They were close to rescuing the buried men, but any added disturbance on the ground, or in the air above the shattered building, could have altered the delicate balance and put his soldiers' lives in danger, as well as spelling disaster for the rescue mission.

'We're almost through,' he said to her, then he nodded to the ambulance attendant who slid the stretcher out of the back of the Land Rover and began to stack equipment they might need onto its lower level.

Kirsten accompanied the orderly back to the building, and saw with relief that a ramp now ran into the room where she and Harry had searched for survivors.

'They're here, both alive!'

A loud cheer greeted the shouted news.

'Stay here, I'm going down,' Harry told Kirsten, and before she could argue that she should see the men before they were shifted, he was gone.

She moved closer, then realised she'd be in the way of someone coming up the flimsy-looking ladder the soldiers had secured to a beam and then slung down into the darkness beneath.

Then Harry's hand appeared, his knuckles white with strain as he gripped the rope and hauled himself upwards. As more of him came into view, she realised why his climb had been so difficult. He was carrying another man slung across his shoulders—his elderly namesake, old Martin Graham.

Kirsten stood back, making room for him to set down his burden, watching the gentleness in the soldier's hands as he lowered the frail old man to the ground.

'We need a stretcher down there for the other man. Doctor, could you see to this chap? My men will bring the other fellow up. He's unconscious but breathing.'

Kirsten needed no second bidding. Grabbing a blanket off the army stretcher, she dropped to her knees beside Mr Graham and smiled reassuringly into his faded brown eyes.

'Is the other man all right? The soldier?' the old man asked, and Kirsten, her hands busy fitting a mask and tube to her emergency oxygen tank, assured him the captain was in good hands.

'I lost my tank when the floor caved in, and the dust down there made me choke,' Mr Graham admitted as Kirsten lifted him to a half-sitting position, propping his back against a lump of masonry, to make breathing easier for him. She slipped the mask across his mouth and nose and adjusted the pressure to deliver a low concentration of oxygen to his lungs.

'You'll be OK now,' Kirsten assured him. 'Just rest. As soon as we've got Jim out, we'll take you up to the hospital.'

She could see two soldiers guiding the ropes as someone

else used the crane's power to haul the stretcher, with the second survivor strapped securely to it, out of the ground.

'Compound fracture of the femur,' the ambulance attendant said to her when he followed the stretcher out of the darkness. 'And possible internal injuries. The major thinks the filing cabinets went through the floor with the two men, and one of them fell on this chap, injuring him with its weight.'

'Can you take him straight up to the helicopter? They'll have an A and E doctor on board who can do more than I can in these circumstances. Explain the man's been trapped underground for some hours, with the possibility of hypothermia to complicate his injuries.'

The ambulance orderly issued orders and the stretcher bearers moved away, but no sooner were they out of earshot than Kirsten remembered she had two patients, not one.

'I should have reminded them to come back for you,' she said, kneeling down again beside Mr Graham. 'But no doubt they will.'

She smiled encouragingly at him.

'And now you've got your breath back, can you answer questions? Are you hurting anywhere? Head, arms, legs, torso? How did you land when you went through the floor? On your feet? Your backside?'

'I'm fine, lassie.' The old man lifted his mask away so he could reply. 'We went down as slowly as a lift in a fancy city building. I only went to the city once and that was a mistake.'

Kirsten heard the echo of sadness in his voice and tucked the blanket more tightly around him. Shock or hypothermia could cause the mind to wander and she guessed that was happening now, although normally he was as mentally alert as a man half his age.

'Although not entirely,' he added, his voice sounding stronger. 'I got Elizabeth, didn't I? And the children.'

Kirsten felt his pulse, fast and erratic. She dug in her bag again and found a juice popper. It wasn't a regular item in a doctor's bag but something she usually carried. She prodded the straw through the hole and handed it to him.

'Here, drink this,' she ordered. He needed fluid faster than the popper would provide, but she wanted him settled in his own bed before she started a drip. If she put one in now, his veins were so fragile that the catheter was likely to tear out when they moved him.

'Why's he still here?'

The major's demand brought her head up with a jerk, and she forgot her concern as she met the glowering look on Harry's face.

'I'm waiting for the ambulance to come back and take him up to the hospital, although if you could organise someone to carry him to my car, we could get going now.'

The glower deepened.

'I don't mean here here, I mean here in Murrawarra.'

Kirsten was battling to make sense of this second demand when the more distant roar of the helicopter's engines told her it was taking off again.

'This is his home,' she said lamely, and was glad when the noise all but drowned out her reply. Not only was she repeating herself, but she knew instinctively that her answer wasn't going to satisfy her inquisitor.

Although something must have got through to him. Two soldiers appeared and, with the major giving what seemed like unnecessary orders about care and gentleness, then taking charge of the oxygen bottle himself, they lifted the old man and carried him across, not to Kirsten's car, but to one of the army vehicles.

'I'll drive him up and help your nurse lift him out at the other end,' he told Kirsten, who was left with no option but to follow in her car.

She saw Mr Graham transferred safely to his room,

started a drip, checked his pulse and blood pressure, switched the tube from his mask to humidified oxygen, again at a low concentration, organised a cup of tea and sandwiches to be delivered to him, then headed, rather wearily, back towards her office.

'He shouldn't be here. He should have gone with the helicopter.'

Harry was standing just inside the door—still glowering.

'I think you made that point earlier,' she retorted. 'But he didn't and that's that. Even if I'd suggested it, he'd have refused, and transporting patients by force has never been my scene.'

She was about to add a few more telling points when she remembered something else. 'That will be up to you to do when you put your grand evacuation plans into place. The enforced removal of sick women and old men from Murrawarra. Where are your super-duper helicopters, anyway? Shouldn't they be here by now?'

He looked uncomfortable, and she could almost imagine a flush beneath the smooth tanned skin of his cheek.

'Our choppers are grounded for the moment,' he grudgingly admitted. 'Fuel problems.'

She began to chuckle, and then to laugh.

Harry looked down at her, torn between wanting to shake her till her teeth rattled and— No, surely he couldn't want to kiss her!

For a start, she was a mess. She had plaster dust whitening the dusky brown curls and smeared all over her clothes. Her shirt was torn, and there was a smear of mud under her left ear.

But her blue eyes shone with merriment, and her lips and cheeks were pink...

'Fuel problems?' she managed to gasp. 'You can't get rid of us because you've got no fuel? How's that for army efficiency?'

He frowned ferociously at her. Shaking her was definitely the option he'd choose—given half a chance!

Though kissing her quiet might work…

'It isn't that we don't have fuel,' he told her stiffly. 'We just can't use it! It's this damnable rain—the flood.'

Now the blue eyes were raised mockingly to his.

'Surely not the flood!' she teased, and he stepped backwards as the temptation to put hands on her, for whatever reason, grew stronger.

'The choppers use a form of high-grade kerosene which is stored in dumps around the country,' he explained with stiff formality. 'Unfortunately, when water gets into these supplies, a microbe called cladisporum can get in between the kerosene and water and it migrates through the fuel and makes gluey blobs which clog the fuel filter—'

'And the helicopter falls out of the sky! What fun!' the cheeky doctor said, still smiling at his discomfort. 'And how long does it take for you to unglue your gluey blobs?'

Her smile had unsettled him to the extent that it took a minute for him to process the question.

'Gluey blobs?' he began vaguely. 'Oh! We don't unglue them—we get new fuel flown in. And before you ask what happens to the bad fuel, I have absolutely no idea. No doubt, someone somewhere has a process for rectifying it.'

Now that cheeky smile grew wider, creating an added sparkle to her eyes.

'Well, tell them not to hurry with the new fuel, as we've no intention of leaving anyway.'

Harry had already guessed that, but it reminded him of something she'd said earlier. Something to do with the old man—

A loud ringing noise halted his mental scan.

'It's Chipper. Sometimes I regret giving him that old doorbell,' Kirsten muttered, then she whisked away, leaving him staring down the passage after her, wondering what he'd wanted to ask.

Something about the closure of the hospital.

He stepped out of her office and looked around. The old man was two doors down. Harry stared in that direction and waited for the frantic beating of his heart to settle slightly.

He would ask about the hospital.

Nothing else.

He took one step, then stopped. Reminded himself he should be checking on his men, or visiting Woulfe if he visited anyone.

He took another step, and stopped again.

The slap of small bare feet on the stone floor broke him out of his indecision. Anthony came hurtling towards him.

'My grandad's back,' he told Harry, seizing his hand and dragging him towards the room. 'Come and meet him, sir. He'd like you. Since my dad died he doesn't have any men to talk to. Only Ken, and he's a nurse so he's always busy and can't stay to chat.'

CHAPTER SIX

'AH, THE army!' The old man greeted him in a voice hoarse with strain, then he nodded towards Anthony. 'Don't let the young scamp get under your feet.'

'I won't!' Anthony protested, settling himself carefully on the edge of the bed and reaching out to touch his grandfather's cheek.

'Are you feeling sick again?' he asked, and the anxiety in his voice caused pain in Harry's chest.

'I'll be better soon, lad. Now, why don't you tell me what you've been doing? Save me talking.'

'Perhaps I could tell you what we plan to do,' Harry suggested. 'Dr McPherson tells me you know the town better than anyone. You don't have to talk, just nod if I get it right and shake your head when I go wrong. I've been working off contour maps but they're not always accurate.'

Was he imagining it, or had the old man's eyes brightened at the suggestion that he could be of use?

Harry began to explain, but soon realised words weren't enough.

'You must have paper and pencils or crayons somewhere,' he said to Anthony. 'How about you run off and get some for me so I can show your grandfather what I mean?'

Anthony obeyed so promptly that Harry realised a few minutes of sitting still was probably all he could manage.

'He seems a good kid,' he said, to fill in time while they waited.

The old man nodded and shifted his mask enough to say, 'He's why I need to stay alive. For a while longer, anyway.'

He reached out and touched Harry's hand. 'Thanks for digging me out today,' he said, then he replaced his mask, closed his eyes and drifted off to sleep.

Harry left the room, anxious to intercept Anthony on his return and stop him waking the patient.

'You still here?' Kirsten asked, meeting him in the passage.

'I'm just leaving,' he told her, feeling edgy because he knew he shouldn't be here—shouldn't have allowed himself to be diverted first by personal emotions, then by a small boy. 'Could you catch Anthony when he comes back and tell him—?'

'You can tell him yourself.' Kirsten touched his arm and pointed towards the front foyer just as Anthony flew off the forbidden banister and landed on the tiled floor. 'When I've done roaring at him for his disobedience.'

Kirsten flung the final words at Harry as she raced towards the child, but Anthony was on his feet and laughing with the sheer exhilaration of his ride before she reached him.

'I should tan your hide, young man!' she scolded. 'You know the rule about not sliding on the banister.'

He turned his meltingly innocent eyes up to hers and said, 'But I was in a hurry. Getting pencils and paper for sir.'

Kirsten surveyed the scattered papers on the foyer floor, then faced the major who was gathering them up.

'I suppose he's too young to recruit?' she asked plaintively.

Harry straightened and smiled at her, making her remember how his body had felt when he'd held her close. How her own had responded. The quivery tremor returned.

'Just a tad,' he said, 'but I'll take him off your hands.' He turned to Anthony. 'Your grandad's gone to sleep so we'll talk to him later. Right now, I've got to drive down town to check on the levee banks. You want to come?'

Kirsten had to bite back an exclamation of surprise. She was certain it would be against army regulations to have a child tagging along on reconnaissance missions, but Anthony looked so delighted she hadn't the heart to spoil things by mentioning it.

Perhaps Harry Graham wasn't as rule-bound as he'd at first appeared.

She didn't see him, or Anthony, again that afternoon, although Bella reported that Anthony had eaten his dinner and gone straight to bed, a sure sign the extra activity had tired him out.

By nine o'clock, all the patients were settled for the night, most of them asleep. Mrs Mathers, evacuated earlier from her house, had been given a room in the east wing, and had instructions to keep Whitey, her raucous cockatoo, covered.

Joan Ryan, the nurse who shared the night duty with Kirsten, was filling out a drug requisition form, using patient files to check off usage against what had been taken from the dispensary.

'You always get the paperwork these days,' Kirsten said, poking her head into the little cubby-hole where the dispensary was housed.

'I like it,' Joan assured her. 'And you know I like night duty, so don't fuss.'

But Kirsten knew she should fuss. Joan had been doing the night shift since the evacuation of the bulk of the town's population ten days earlier. While she hadn't been rushed off her feet and had been able to sleep most nights, it was still a bad policy to allow staff to miss days off.

Not that there was anything to do on days off—just walk down to look at the water, or hang around the building— so even the day staff had opted for a regime of working when there was work to do, and resting, reading or watching TV, thankfully still available via satellite, when there wasn't.

Noises from the kitchen suggested they were all in there, gathered, as they were most nights, for a late supper and a bit of socialising before they went off to the little cell-like rooms they'd made their temporary homes since the decision had been made for the staff to live in during the emergency.

Should she go and join them? She usually did, if only for a short time. But tonight a restlessness sent her feet in the opposite direction, out through the foyer to stand under the portico and breathe fresh air.

'At least the rain's stopped.'

The male voice startled her, and she spun around to see Harry leaning against one of the pillars.

'I suppose that's something,' she said. 'It will make it slightly less difficult for your men if we get some fine days.'

'It would also make it easier to move your patients,' he reminded her.

She smiled in the darkness, for his words lacked their former conviction.

'You don't sound nearly as determined about that as you did earlier. Is it because you can't get the transport, with your fuel problem, or that you're having second thoughts?'

He didn't answer and she searched the shadowy outline of his face but couldn't read anything in the darkness.

'Second, third and fourth thoughts,' he admitted. 'Tell me why it's so important for you to stay.' He moved closer to her and took her arm to steer her towards an old wooden garden seat, left behind by the previous tenants.

'It keeps coming into conversations,' he added as they both sat down. 'As if evacuation was equated with closure of the hospital.'

Kirsten turned from her survey of the flood waters—silver in the hazy moonlight, stretching as far as she could see—and studied the man beside her.

'It is,' she said bluntly. 'After the second flood, the Health Department decided it would be more economic to close the hospital altogether than to rebuild. I don't know how much you know of the dynamics of a country town, but closing the hospital is like a death sentence. It's the beginning of the end for a town like Murrawarra.'

'But Vereton is only a little over an hour away—when the roads are open. Many city people have to travel a couple of hours to reach a hospital.'

Kirsten sighed. It was an argument she'd heard often enough but it never failed to irritate her.

'But they probably have a doctor in their local shopping centre, and X-ray facilities in a nearby mall, not to mention pathology labs, access to a variety of therapists, natural health clinics and ancillary services from paediatric to geriatric. Out here, all that comes with the hospital. It goes, the doctor goes—'

'You're fighting for your job?'

Irritation sent Kirsten to her feet. It was that or poke him in the chest again, and she had a feeling that the less close she was to him the better she could think—and argue.

'I can get a job anywhere,' she told him huffily. 'But not in Murrawarra, so one person leaves town. Normally, we've a staff of thirty full or part time connected with the hospital, and if you add up their dependants that's another sixty-eight people who would be directly affected by the hospital closure. If they leave town to find employment elsewhere, they take twenty children from the school and that's one teacher less it requires.'

'So it's a domino effect, with every family leaving town reducing the need for services.'

Kirsten was pleased he understood but she was too wound up to stop now.

'And that's before you get to the people who leave because they need the hospital,' she told him. 'The elderly who can't travel, young families with children at risk, people who suffer from unpredictable conditions like asthma or diabetes or epilepsy.'

'But surely you can't keep the hospital open without government funding? If the bean-counters have decided it's to close, aren't you fighting a losing battle?'

His reminder of the reality of the situation stopped Kirsten's feet and she glared at him.

'You're suggesting we just give in? Lie down and let them steamroll right over us? Is that the way the army plans its campaigns? Do you say, oh, we can't win this little war, so we won't fight it?'

He stood up and grasped her shoulders.

'Hey, calm down,' Harry said, then he smiled. 'Yes, we would go into a battle that might look impossible, but not before we'd considered a strategy to limit the odds against us. Not before we'd studied the opposition, summed up its strengths and sought out its weaknesses, and worked out what plan of attack would give us the best chance of success.'

Kirsten looked into his face, less shadowed now they were in the cloud-filtered moonlight. His dark eyes looked intently into hers, and somewhere in her brain she knew his words were making sense—telling her something important.

But she couldn't grasp the essence of it because other thoughts, born of sensation, were jostling it away. She stepped backwards, out from under the hands that had remained, resting lightly, on her shoulders. She dragged air into her all but paralysed lungs, and told herself attraction didn't work that way. Not so quickly and completely.

Not real attraction.

It must be physical, this thing she felt.

Possibly the result of too long without a significant other in her life—

'You said if the hospital closed and you had to leave town, that was one person gone.' Harry's voice jolted through her denial. 'Does that mean you're single—no significant other in your life?'

'Snap!' she muttered to herself, and she turned away from him, wanting to run back inside, to seek refuge in her room—though she suspected a different environment wouldn't provide a refuge from her thoughts.

'Why?' Kirsten asked out loud when she'd rejected running like a scalded cat.

'Why what?' he asked, stepping close again—looking puzzled.

'Why ask about significant others?'

Harry frowned down at her.

'Did I ask that?' he demanded, and she began to think he was as confused as she was.

Perhaps a change in conversation would help them both.

'The staff have supper in the kitchen each evening if your men would like to join in,' she said.

'They have a mess but, yes, some combined activity might be beneficial. We could be here for a month after the water recedes, depending on the damage.'

A month after the water recedes?

Her thoughts flitted like a moth from this revelation, to touch down lightly on attraction, bypass drawing up battle plans to save the hospital and finally settle on a very large mental warning sign some still sane part of her brain had erected.

Fortunately, at that moment she heard a bell ringing inside.

'They're playing my song,' she said, pretending a lightness she was far from feeling. 'Chipper, I'd say. He falls asleep and gets tangled in his weights and pulleys.'

She walked towards the door as she delivered this explanation, but escape evaded her for Harry walked right alongside her.

'How did he break his pelvis—a fall of some kind?'

Kirsten chuckled as the reminder of Chipper's accident brought her back down to earth.

'Would you believe rough riding?' she asked as they entered the shadowy foyer. 'He was a professional rodeo rider at one time and the silly old coot was trying to explain to a new chum how to hook his fingers around the rope. The youngster couldn't follow the instructions so Chipper climbs onto the bull—it's still in the chute—to demonstrate. Someone opens the gate, the bull roars out and throws Chipper straight into the air. He was so astonished he forgot to hold on, and came down hard on his backside—one broken pelvis.'

Harry chuckled his delight, the sound so seductive it undid all the good telling him about Chipper had done.

'I'd love to have been there,' he said weakly when he'd regained control.

'So would half the town,' Kirsten told him, walking down the passage towards Chipper's room.

She was about to grasp the doorknob when it swung away from her and Joan stood in the light thrown by Chipper's bedside lamp.

'It's not Chipper,' Joan explained. 'I pressed his bell to get you here because I didn't want Mr Graham fretting. I don't like his colour and his breathing's very raspy.'

'Delayed shock?' Kirsten thought aloud. 'Not to mention the dust he must have inhaled. Thanks, Joan. I'll go in and see him.'

'What exactly's wrong with him?'

Kirsten spun around, belatedly realising Harry was still with her.

'He has permanent and irreversible damage to the alveoli, the little pouches in the lungs where the exchange of gases from the lungs to the bloodstream takes place. We can get oxygen in by increasing the percentage of oxygen in the air he breathes, but it's getting the carbon dioxide out that causes problems.'

She tapped on the patient's door as she finished this explanation and pushed it open. The blueness around the old man's lips told its own story.

'Not too good?' she asked gently, and saw his rueful grimace.

'I'd like to put you on the respirator, if only overnight,' she said, and realised how bad he must be feeling when he nodded his agreement.

She left the room, passed Harry in the passage and walked to the storeroom where the respirator was kept.

'What's it for?' Harry had followed her again.

'It will essentially breathe for him. We have another machine that provides intermittent positive pressure, cutting off when the set pressure in the lungs is achieved and allowing him to exhale through a valve, but that's used more for short periods of time to help clean out the lungs. Because his experience today has left him weak, I'd prefer he went on the respirator for the night.'

'Why doesn't he use it all the time?'

Kirsten closed her eyes then opened them to ask, 'Does the army teach you to question everything? Or are you mechanically minded that you have to know? Mr Graham doesn't like using it because he believes it would worry the children to see him hooked up to a machine.'

'That's stupid. Everyone knows children are adaptable,' Harry growled at her.

'You'd know, would you?' Kirsten asked, disturbed by the trend of this conversation. 'Have some of your own?'

'No, I don't, but I read that somewhere,' the major asserted.

She refused to acknowledge the flutter of relief she felt, and wheeled the pump and the oxygen tank that fed it into Mr Graham's room. Then she plugged it in to the power socket and set the dials. Joan came in with a tray containing a mild topical anaesthetic, a lubricant and a choice of endotracheal tubes.

'I'll connect it to a nasotracheal tube,' Kirsten told Mr Graham. 'You'll be more comfortable that way.'

More comfortable than what? she thought as she prepared the tube then slid it into place. Once it was down, she listened to his chest to check it was properly positioned, then taped it into place, before connecting it to the respirator.

'Will you stay with him, Joan?' she asked the nurse. 'Check the patency of the tube in thirty minutes, BP every hour and suction his trachea every hour as well. Actually, I'll be back by then so I can take over.'

She left the room and turned towards her office, wanting to check an article she'd read in a recent magazine about intermittent positive pressure breathing versus the volume respirator. Perhaps by morning she could take Mr Graham off the respirator and use the IPPB unit for fifteen minutes at intervals during the day.

'Will he be all right?'

The question was asked in a harsh whisper but still startled Kirsten enough to cause panic heartbeats.

'Don't you ever go to bed?' she demanded in an infuriated undertone. 'Or, having failed to get us airlifted out, have you decided to frighten us all to death?'

'I'd been outside, checking the camp, and was coming back in when I saw you coming out of his room.'

Harry seemed genuinely concerned, perhaps because he'd been involved in rescuing the old man, and Kirsten relented.

'Come in,' she said, pushing open the door, 'but you'll have to work for your information this time. There's an electric kettle over there on the cupboard. I'll have a black coffee, two sugars, and help yourself to what you want while I look something up.'

He was no sooner in than she regretted her invitation. The room was large enough, but it was her bedroom as well as her office and the man seemed to impose his presence on it in a way none of the staff ever did.

Ignoring the stupid fancy, she riffled through her pile of half-read professional journals and papers until she found the article she wanted. Then she turned on the desk light and sat down to refresh her mind on the outcome of some tests carried out on the far side of the world.

'Therapeutic IPPB,' she mumbled to herself, pleased to find she'd remembered correctly. 'For up to thirty minutes four times a day. Use a mouthpiece and nose clip to ensure optimum results.'

'Coffee.'

The cup of coffee landed on the desk and was pushed tentatively towards her.

'Did you find what you wanted?'

She looked up at Harry and smiled.

'Yes, I did, and thanks for the coffee. Sorry to treat you like that but something was nagging at me.'

He smiled back and again Kirsten felt an uneasy sense of invasion at this man's presence in her room.

'Well, are you going to share it?' he prodded, propping himself on a corner of the desk.

'I'm going to try some different inhalation therapy on Mr Graham tomorrow,' she announced. 'Up to now he hasn't really been a patient although from time to time he's been admitted to hospital for treatment for an infection or occasionally when his carbon dioxide retention levels have risen and caused other problems. Now that he's a real patient, I'm going to give this system a go. See if it leads to an improvement in his general health.'

'Poor man! All he wanted to do was help out in the floods and now you have him at your mercy!'

Harry's brown eyes gleamed down into hers and she knew he was teasing her, but she didn't want Harry Graham teasing her any more than she wanted his image imprinted in her room.

And as for gleaming brown eyes...

She closed her own against their appeal and an image of faded brown eyes was superimposed upon them.

'Why are you so interested in Mr Graham?' she asked. 'Because you share a surname? Are you related? Do you think you might be?'

The gleam faded and his eyelids, fringed by thick black lashes, dropped to hide his thoughts.

'I'm interested in Chipper, too, and Moira and her motor neurone disease.'

'But what about Captain Woulfe?' Kirsten persisted. 'I doubt you've so much as visited him.'

The eyelashes fluttered upwards again and a spark flashed in the darkness.

'Shows how much you know. I'd been sitting with him for half an hour before we met outside. Then your young nurse—Mary, is she? She came back in her civvies with a pack of cards and some board games, and I felt my presence was no longer required.'

'Hmm,' Kirsten said, thinking more of Mary and the young captain than of Harry's protestations.

And he'd shifted the conversation from Mr Graham, and probably thought she'd missed the switch. She studied him for a moment, wondering if she'd let him get away with it, thinking, on another level, what strong facial bones he had. A sculpted look that projected strength.

And reliability.

And a masculine appeal!

A shiver shafted through her. Masculine appeal indeed. The man would be gone in a month, possibly less if the water went down more quickly than was predicted.

'Where do you come from?' she asked, the question a logical extension of her thoughts, although they were more concerned with where he'd go to. Perhaps not the same thing.

'Melbourne originally, though I'm based at Holdsworthy in New South Wales now.'

He shifted off her desk and took a turn around the room, but something in the way he looked suggested he was distracted—not seeing it at all.

'And is the army your life? Are you there until they pin a long-service medal on you and retire you honourably from the service?'

He swung back to face her, and frowned as if the question had interrupted some other train of thought.

'I haven't considered getting out,' he said, 'although I guess it's always an option—should something else come along.'

'Something else like what?' she asked, and refused to consider why she was in the least bit interested in Harry Graham's future.

He smiled and shrugged the broad shoulders she'd admired more than once today.

'I don't know,' he said, but he spoke slowly, as if he wasn't certain he was telling the truth.

Harry watched the doctor lift her cup and drain the last of her coffee. He sensed she was about to leave the room— or ask him to go—but more than anything he wanted to talk to her, to sound her out about the dilemma now facing him.

But how? He could hardly blurt out a condensed version of his life story—particularly the details of an irrepressible, energetic, city-loving mother—to a woman he'd only just met.

'I'm going back to sit with Mr Graham,' she said, proving his instinct right.

'Why you?' he demanded, upset that she should have to do this when she'd already had a long, traumatic day.

She smiled, and he saw the dancing lights in the mesmeric blue eyes and almost forgot his question.

'Because I want to,' she told him. 'While he's on the respirator he needs suctioning, and his lips and mouth require moistening. His pulse and blood pressure have to be checked, the tube watched to ensure it doesn't slip or close on itself. These are things night staff do automatically in a normal hospital situation, but with limited night staff I'd just as soon leave Joan free for the other patients—Cathy's baby will wake for feeds, your soldier will need turning—while I stay with Mr Graham.'

It seemed reasonable but didn't make him feel any better about her sitting up all night.

'Couldn't you sedate him? I thought that's what hospitals did with their patients at night?'

'Only if they want to attract law suits,' she said, the smile sparkling in her eyes again. 'And with Mr Graham, sedation is the worst possible suggestion. Even mild sedation can depress the respiratory system—definitely contra-indicated in his condition.'

Definitely contra-indicated.

The phrase echoed in Harry's head, only his mind was using it to warn him against involvement in this town—this hospital—with either the patients or the staff.

Kirsten pushed back her chair and stood up, the top of

her head barely reaching his shoulder. As she leant over to turn out the desk lamp he saw the dark shadows beneath her eyes and again considered what she'd been through today.

'I could sit with your patient if you showed me what to do,' he offered.

'You'd be no use at all to your troops tomorrow if you did. You've got a bigger job ahead of you than I have,' she reminded him, and the gentle smile that accompanied the words made his head swim.

And suddenly he wanted to answer the question she'd asked earlier—about his future in the army.

The army's been my family, he wanted to explain. Provided a stability I'd never known. Been there for me when I had no one else.

But he knew it would sound weak, even pathetic, and, until today, he hadn't known it mattered. Which was something else he had to think through before he discussed it with anyone.

Kirsten waited for Harry to take the hint and leave her room, but he'd gone back to pacing again and she wondered what was disturbing him so much that he couldn't stand still.

'I'm off now,' she said, hoping this time he'd catch on. But he nodded absent-mindedly and continued pacing.

What harm could he do? she asked herself, opening the door and stepping out into the corridor.

'Goodnight,' he said, the politeness that shone through all his dealings still very much to the fore.

'And goodnight to you, Harry Graham,' she said, then she grinned at him. 'But that's not your room. It's mine. Haven't you got a tent to go to? A nice camp stretcher of your own?'

He looked so startled she had to chuckle, mirth gurgling through her at the comical expression on his face.

'I was distracted,' he said gruffly, pushing past her and striding down the passage. 'And I'm not sleeping in a tent,' he added, pausing and turning back to face her. 'You offered us the first floor and the east wing, in case you don't remember. Not that there's much difference between a nun's cell and an army tent.'

He spun around again and continued on his way.

Not much difference, Kirsten thought as she walked back to Mr Graham's room. Was he talking about the loneliness of command?

Or was he telling her something else?

Something that harked back to his question about a significant other in her life—to her question about whether he had children?

Was he hinting at celibacy?

A man who looked like Harry Graham?

Her head scoffed at the idea, but her heart didn't mind it.

Not a bit of temporary celibacy.

Recent temporary celibacy.

She grinned at her stupid thoughts and went quietly in to where her patient lay sleeping, though doubtless uncomfortably.

'I'll sit with him,' she whispered to Joan, lifting the newly written-up chart from the foot of the bed and carrying it to the corner where a dim light burned above an easy chair.

'I'll bring you in a hot drink in a couple of hours,' Joan promised, and she tiptoed from the room.

Satisfied with Joan's obs, Kirsten set the chart back in place, then sat down. While she was observing him and listening to his breathing sounds, she could allow a longer interval between suctioning which would give her patient more uninterrupted sleep.

And she'd give some thought to Harry's contention that

the army sought to know the enemy and made up its battle plans accordingly. What Murrawarra needed was a long-term strategy to fight the hospital closure, not the piecemeal skirmishes they'd conducted so far.

Perhaps if he was going to be around for a month, he'd help them plan...

CHAPTER SEVEN

BY SIX next morning Mr Graham was feeling better, the flood waters had risen another two feet and the rain had returned as a slow and monotonous drizzle.

Kirsten visited all her patients, then handed over to Ken while she caught up on some sleep. She set the alarm as she wanted to start Mr Graham on the IPPB unit at eight. That way she could fit in four sessions in the day. As she drifted off to sleep she realised she'd have to read the article again. She had no idea how long it would be before she could expect to see any improvement.

Waking at two-thirty had not been part of the plan, and she only knew it was two-thirty because, after failing to find her clock when she turned sleepily towards where it should have been, she checked her watch.

She sprang out of bed, dragged on the first clothes she could find and careered out into the passage, seeking Ken and considering murder.

'Calm down!' he told her, actually reaching out to hold her steady while she all but danced in frustration. 'I put Mr Graham on the machine at eight and again at twelve. You'd told me that was the plan when I came on duty.'

'You took my clock!' she spluttered, and he had the temerity to smile at her.

'Actually, I didn't. The army took it!' he told her. 'It was the major's idea to let you sleep. He said you were probably too stubborn to realise you'd need a decent sleep to get over the stress you'd been through yesterday.'

'He took my clock? He went into my room and stole my clock?'

Ken grinned again.

'Well, I wasn't game enough to do it so he had to,' he said.

Kirsten wrenched herself away from him and stormed off down the passage.

'Just wait until I find him. The cheek of him! If he thinks he can run my hospital he's got another think coming. I'll—'

Ken caught her from behind and stopped her headlong rush.

'I wouldn't go rushing out there like that,' he said mildly. 'Most of the men will be down at the levee bank but there'll be some around the camp.'

Kirsten looked down at herself.

She'd pulled on the filthy jeans she'd worn the previous day, and on top a khaki shirt so worn she now used it as a duster. What it had been doing on the floor near her jeans she had no idea.

And to make matters worse, it was buttoned all wrong so the material was bunched up, giving views of skin and the edge of one breast to anyone who happened to glance her way.

Her cheeks heated with mortification and she slunk back to her room, found clean clothes, then headed for the bathroom she'd set aside for staff, up the stairs on the first floor.

Fate, not working with her at the moment, decreed that Harry Graham should be descending the stairs as she ascended. She clutched her towel and bundle of clean clothes closer to her chest to hide the misbuttoned shirt and glimpses of skin, and frowned ferociously at him.

'I want a word with you later,' she growled.

He seemed unfazed by her wrath—even had the hide to smile.

'About Peter?' he said blithely. 'I've already set him up with a job. And I dug out some recruiting material that was in my briefcase from a previous trip. Something for him to read and consider.'

As well as yelling at him for stealing her clock, she should have said thank you and then explained that Peter's fussy mother would never let him join up, but his cheery attitude left her speechless and by the time she'd sorted out the priorities in her reply he was gone.

Neither did he reappear all day, or materialise in the dimly lit passageway that night.

It was the return of the rain that was making her feel depressed, Kirsten told herself as she sat at her desk a day later—the day before the floods were due to peak—writing up her notes and hardly daring to believe that things could be going as well as they were. Mr Graham was definitely a lot better, Cathy and the baby, now blessed with the name of Robert, junior, were blooming, Chipper was his normal self, Mr Curtis almost with it and even Moira was having a good day.

'It's the calm before the storm,' she told Peggy, who appeared with a tray containing a pot of tea and sandwiches and announced that Bella had sent lunch to save her going to the kitchen.

'Nonsense,' Peggy said. 'It's your organisation that's got it all running so well, and now the army's here you don't have to be worrying so much about the civilians down there in town. That must make it easier for you.'

Kirsten thanked her for the lunch tray but refused to agree with her contention that the army had somehow miraculously improved the condition of her patients.

Although she had to admit it had helped Peter Phelps. In a cautious foray into his room earlier, she'd found him sitting up in bed, not counting paper-clips but drawing in the buildings in the main street on a contour map of Murrawarra.

'I've got to do this, then do the outlying area, colouring

in the properties where people have stayed on, so the major knows who's where,' he'd told Kirsten proudly. 'I have to phone the farms and make sure someone *is* there, and later, when the major's worked out an evacuation plan, I have to let them know about it.'

It had seemed logical and reasonable to Kirsten, but she assumed that the major, who was fast achieving god-like status among the convent's inmates, would have had someone on his staff equally able to do the job. She had to give him full marks for co-operation as far as Peter was concerned.

Relieved of worries, she phoned Vereton Hospital for a report on Jim Thompson, only to find he'd been transferred on to the city for surgery on his leg. After some general chat about other Murrawarra patients at present in the town, she was about to hang up when the medical officer in charge put her on hold.

'The area manager wanted a word,' he explained, coming back on the line a few seconds later. 'I just had to check he was available. I'm switching you through now.'

Kirsten's heart sank and she could have sworn the day grew cloudier, the rain heavier. Hal Burton, the area manager, was like a dark shadow in her life.

'Hi, Hal. How's everything with you?' she asked brightly, while her mind was wondering just how soon she'd get an opportunity to pick Harry Graham's brain about strategic planning.

Hal's voice quacked on at her, exchanging pleasantries at first, then going for the jugular.

'The insurance claim you put in was most irregular,' he said with infuriating pomposity.

'Nonsense!' Kirsten refused to concede a point in her arguments with the man. 'The building is the property of the hospital board, so they were entitled to claim on their insurance.'

'The hospital has come under the state government umbrella for many years now,' Hal reminded her.

'Yes, the hospital has,' Kirsten granted, 'but we're talking about the building here.'

'The building *is* the hospital. Without it you don't have a hospital and, in fact, you haven't a building now—have you? Not a proper hospital building.'

She had to clench her jaw to keep her voice even, and the fingers holding the receiver were shaking with the effort to control her temper.

'We have a perfect building—far better than the old one—and, as I've pointed out to you before, Hal, the word ''hospital'' to my mind covers the range of services provided, not a physical place.'

There was a soft tap on the door and it opened a few inches, enough for Harry Graham to poke his head through the gap.

'Oh, you're busy. I'll come back,' he said softly, but Kirsten realised this was too good an opportunity to miss and beckoned him urgently inside.

Her inattention meant she missed what Hal was saying, but she knew she wouldn't have liked it, or agreed with it, so she didn't ask him to repeat it.

It was when he added 'So don't expect the usual transfer of funds at the beginning of the quarter' that she again sat up and took notice.

'I've staff to pay,' she protested. 'And patients to treat. You can't do that!'

'Oh, can't I?' he said, and she could almost see the smirk over the phone.

She slammed the phone back into its cradle and wiped her hands on her jeans.

'Slimy bastard!' she muttered, glaring at the phone as if it might somehow transmit her rage to the area manager's office.

'Trouble?' Harry said, settling his hip on her desk and looking as if he'd come to stay.

'Don't you ever have work to do?' she grumbled at him. 'Or is the army such a well-oiled machine it doesn't need its leaders?'

'Hey, you asked me in!' he protested, looking affronted, although she was sure she could see laughter in his lovely eyes.

She could *definitely* feel her now familiar internal reaction to his presence.

'You were there already,' she reminded him, then remembered exactly why she'd asked him in. 'Have you got a minute?'

He burst into laughter, the deep, rich sound rumbling up through his chest.

'First you have a go at me for not doing enough work, and now you want to take me from my duties—no doubt to help you in some patient-support scheme. I've already organised young Phelps.'

Kirsten, finding his closeness was doing funny things to the nerve endings in her skin, pushed her chair back from the desk.

'Yes, I know, and I'm very grateful,' she said, hoping she sounded suitably humble. 'But there's something else I wanted to ask you. About what you said the other day. About strategies. And planning. And learning the enemy's weaknesses.'

'That's three somethings,' he told her, but she guessed, from the intent look on his face, that she had his attention.

'So far we've been fighting the hospital closure a bit at a time, but you're right. We need a plan. Need to be organised. How do we do it?' she asked. 'Where do we start?'

His dark brows tugged together as he frowned down at her from his superior perch on the desk.

'I don't know much about the dynamics of small towns.

Or things like how big a population the pen-pushers in this state require before they agree a hospital is viable. Is distance from a major centre taken into account? So many questions and considerations. I don't see how I could help you.'

'You know about plans,' Kirsten told him, refusing to allow a little initial disappointment to put her off. 'About strategies. We need a strategy.'

She looked earnestly, and appealingly, up into his face, hoping he wouldn't remember how rude she'd been to him on previous occasions.

The frown vanished as he smiled at her.

'I'll have to think about this,' he teased. 'Especially about the change in attitude from Murrawarra's doctor. Going from being the bad guy to the good guy so suddenly is disconcerting to say the least.'

Of course he'd remembered. She bit her lip to stop a cutting retort, and shrugged his remark away.

'Things have been a bit fraught,' she said, as casually as she could.

But the devil wouldn't let the matter rest. The glint of mischief in his eyes told Kirsten that much.

'I figured that,' he said smoothly. 'But it was self-inflicted, wouldn't you say? I mean, if you'd gone along with the official evacuation—'

'I knew you'd bring that up again!' Kirsten fumed, giving up all pretence at being nice. 'You just had to say "I told you so", didn't you?'

And once again his laughter rang through her room.

'I wondered how long it would take you to crack,' he teased. 'Boy! You had a go at me about a change of clothes improving my temper—perhaps it's time you slipped into something more comfortable.'

Kirsten knew he hadn't meant it the way the phrase was

usually used, but it struck her that way and she felt the heat of total embarrassment wash up into her cheeks.

Harry saw her eyes darken and her cheeks turn pink, and realised what he'd inadvertently said. He was sorry he'd embarrassed her, but had no idea how to extricate himself from the mess he'd made of what had been a teasing conversation.

'I'll think about strategies and plans,' he said, standing up because his body was reacting to his earlier words and her scarlet cheeks, regretting he had to somehow retract them. It seemed to think Dr McPherson in something more comfortable would be most appealing. 'I'll see you later.'

He walked towards the door then remembered what he'd come to ask and spun back.

'How's Mr Graham?' he asked. 'Did the night on the respirator help him? Did the intermittent therapy improve his condition? Could I—?'

He stopped, his body's confusion forgotten as mental confusion took over. He hadn't intended asking if he could visit the old man, although he wanted to talk to him, to learn more about him.

'Could you what?' Kirsten seemed to have recovered from her confusion, and was now eyeing him assessingly.

Would she find the question odd? Wonder about his motives?

'Pop in and see him some time,' Harry managed to say, then, in the hope it would make his request sound even more casual, he added, 'Anthony was saying his grandfather enjoys male company.'

'I'm still putting him on the machine four-hourly—that's at four and again at eight. Any other time, if he's awake, yes, I'm sure he'd welcome company.'

She sounded distracted and he hoped it was because she was thinking of her patient's health, not his reasons for wanting to visit. Although he knew eventually, if he decided—no, before he decided—he'd have to discuss it with her.

Kirsten watched the door close behind her disturbing visitor. If she wanted his help, working out a plan to keep the hospital open, she'd have to stop reacting to every casual comment he made and, if possible, stop her body going haywire whenever he settled close to her.

The rest of the day passed without interruption. In fact, it was so quiet that in the late afternoon, when the rain eased off and a weak sunshine struggled through the clouds, she found the children and suggested they all take a walk downtown to see where the water was and how the men were faring on the levee bank.

'Mum says it's much higher out at home,' Libby told her as they made their way down the hill. 'She's moved all the chickens into the house in case it comes up that high, but in all Grandad's records it's never gone into the henhouse.'

'I hope Bessie's all right, and Suds and Soapy,' Meg added, mentioning the family cat and the two dogs who'd remained at the farm.

'They'll be all right,' Anthony said. 'Suds and Soapy, they can swim better than I can, and Bessie can climb on the roof if it comes too close.'

'But Mum couldn't climb on the roof,' Libby, who was the worrier of the family, put in.

'We'll get her out if it looks as if it will go into the house,' Kirsten assured her. 'And we should know that today or at the latest tomorrow. The men can tell how high it will go from how fast it's rising and how high it was at the towns upstream.'

'Will she be able to bring the pets?' Anthony asked. 'And the chickens?'

The army was now officially in charge of the locals' safety and Kirsten wasn't sure how Harry would feel, fer-

rying a stranded woman, with one cat, two dogs and mul-
titudinous chickens, back to the town.

'The water won't go right over the house,' she said, 'so
the chickens could sit on the roof if they had to.'

This seemed to satisfy the children, who switched the
conversation to how long they might be able to skip school,
given that the school buildings were already partially submerged and doubtless would take some renovating once the
flood receded.

They had reached a point on the road just above where
the main street had been and were looking towards the
school when Meg grasped her arm.

'There's someone in the water,' Meg said. 'Over by the
school. Look! Look!'

Meg's cry was drowned out by a loud shout from the
other side of the main street.

Kirsten looked, and as more and more voices were raised
in panic and alarm and a carrying voice began yelling orders, she realised what had happened. A section of the levee
bank had given way and, whether by sheer bad luck or
because the men *were* working there, the rush of water had
carried a number of the workers into the floods.

'Stay right here,' she said to the children. 'Libby, you're
in charge.'

She left them and raced in the direction the flow of water
was taking. A couple of men had already grabbed onto the
tops of trees or parts of buildings and were clinging tight
to their makeshift anchors, but Kirsten had seen that first
body float past, carried so limply in the swirling water that
she knew the person must either be dead or unconscious.

Working out where it would come closest to shore, she
stayed on dry land for as long as possible, only diving in
when houses blocked her way and diverted the soldier—
she could make out his fatigues—away from her.

Behind her she could hear the splutter of a boat engine

kicking to life and she knew the other men would soon be plucked from their perilous perches. But if they got to this man too late—or hadn't missed him yet...

Her arms cut through the water, while debris bashed against her body. He was close—so close—but the water swept him on. Taking a last look in his direction, and a lungful of air, she stuck her head down and put on a mammoth spurt, not stopping until she felt cloth and softness and knew she'd reached him.

She lowered her feet, hoping she might find something solid underneath her, but they were well down the main street now, the tops of telegraph poles mocking her as she was swept past.

She grasped the man under the arms and dragged him under to turn his body so when they both surfaced he was face up. It was Lt Ross, his face ashen white, except for a bloody gash across his right temple. Pedalling her legs furiously to stay afloat, she turned his head and forced three quick breaths into his lungs. Impossible to tell if he was breathing on his own, but she couldn't take the chance he wasn't.

Clutching him to her, she peered ahead, working out where the next telegraph pole was—and how close the water would carry them to it.

She could hear shouts behind her, men calling to each other—or to their rescuers— but right now she had to keep getting air into the lieutenant's lungs. The pole came closer, the crossbars on it less than a foot above flood level. She flung out her free hand and felt it smack against the bar, then she curled her arm around it and clung tight. Wires ripped from their moorings by floating debris now whipped against their bodies, but she ignored them and held on.

'Now all I have to do is get you over it,' she told her unconscious patient. 'Hang on!'

Propping him against the pole, she once again went under water, needing the buoyancy to help her lift his weight. She braced her feet against the pole, her shoulders under James's chest, and heaved, sending her limp burden catapulting over the crossbar.

It must have been the jolting of his diaphragm against the bar that cleared his lungs because, as Kirsten emerged from the water, she heard a cough and saw her rescued soldier bring up a gallon or so of flood water and what was probably the remnants of his lunch.

She hauled her upper body over the bar to join him, and held him when feebly protesting movements threatened to tip him off.

'Stay still,' she told him. 'Someone will come. I thought you were dead, you know. You scared me silly.'

He groaned and retched weakly, then muttered something about feeling like death, but Kirsten could see his chest moving and knew he was breathing and right now that was all she cared about. She held onto him, keeping him pinned to the bar while the waters tugged at their legs and sucked at their lower bodies, tempting them to slide back in.

The soldiers would have had a roll call by now. They'd have missed Lt Ross. Soon someone would come.

Kirsten told herself that when the sound of the boat engine grew more distant rather than closer.

'They're ferrying the other people they've rescued back to dry ground,' she told James as she wriggled around so she could press a balled-up handkerchief over the bleeding cut.

She listened for the motors to start up again—for the boat that was coming closer.

Couldn't hear it.

'Soon. They'll come soon.' She said it out loud this time to reassure herself, but it was another half-hour before she heard the roar of an outboard. A half-hour in which her arms had gone numb, and James had lost consciousness a couple of times.

'Determined to make a nuisance of yourself, Doctor?'

Kirsten was so relieved to see the aluminium dinghy coming towards them that she ignored the jibe.

'He's fading in and out of consciousness. If you try to get close upstream you could wedge us both against the pole, so could you come around downstream of us, then I'll let him drop and you can grab him?' she said, and gained momentary satisfaction from the sudden shock on Harry's face.

'*He's* unconscious. You've rescued him, not he you?'

'What did you think I was doing?' Grouchiness at the disbelief in his tone swallowed the satisfaction. 'Taking a swim? Trying out for the Olympics?'

Then Harry was there beside her, his strong arms holding her pinned against the bar while he somehow manoeuvred James's limp body off and into the boat.

'Now you, sunshine!' he said, but once again reaction set in and Kirsten began to shake so badly she'd have fallen into the water if Harry hadn't held her safe. She turned and clung to him, although in some deep recess of her mind she knew that was stupid. It meant he was holding the weight of both of them above water.

But he didn't try to ease her off or dump her unceremoniously over the bar, as she had done to James. He tightened his arm around her and let his body feed its warmth into hers until the shivering lessened slightly.

'We'll have to travel together,' he said to the men in the boat. 'Take Lt Ross back to dry land and hand him over to the medics then come straight back for us.'

'Why did you send them away?' Kirsten asked him, her teeth chattering so badly she could barely get the words out.

'Because you're holding on to me and we wouldn't both

fit in the boat. I couldn't work out how to get you in without me going too, and probably capsizing it.'

He didn't like her holding onto him, Kirsten decided, but, try as she may, she couldn't let go.

In the end he peeled her hands off him, but only while he passed her down into the boat. Then he dropped in himself, got settled on the seat and wrapped her in a blanket, before holding her tight again, apparently unconcerned by what his soldiers thought of such behaviour.

'Body heat's the best way of warming someone,' he said when she made a feeble effort to move away. 'I'm sure one of the men cuddled James as they ferried him back ashore.'

Kirsten blinked the water from her eyes and looked at her rescuer. He was studying her as if trying to understand her better.

'You've got to stop getting involved in these rescue missions,' he scolded gently.

'I didn't know if you'd seen him go into the water. Actually, it was Meg who spotted him, and he wasn't struggling—swimming—making any attempt to save himself.'

'So you plunged in,' Harry said, and Kirsten imagined she could hear a little admiration as well as censure in his voice. 'Lucky for you both that the children were with you. Ross must have come down with a message. He wasn't part of the detail so he wasn't missed. It was only the children saying you were in the water that made me take the boat out again to look.'

The engine noise stopped suddenly so Harry's final words were unnecessarily loud. As a cheer went up from the shore Kirsten pushed herself away from his warm body and belatedly ran a hand through her hair, wondering if she looked as wet and bedraggled as she felt.

'Like something the cat dragged in,' Harry told her, reading her thoughts and confirming her fears. 'Get in the Land

Rover and I'll have someone drive you up the hill. You're the one who needs a change of clothes today.'

Kirsten looked around. The three children were clustered near the vehicles, perhaps told by Harry to wait right there.

'Where's James?' she asked, and saw Harry's dark eyes darken slightly before thick lashes concealed his expression.

Should she have called the youngster Lt Ross?

'The ambulance will have taken him. The medics will contact you if they feel he needs more attention than they can provide, although if there's the slightest risk of complications I want him flown out.'

Kirsten allowed herself to be helped from the dinghy, then she crossed, still wrapped in the army blanket, towards the children.

'Come on, kids. Back up the hill.'

They climbed into the Land Rover without argument, perhaps sobered by what had happened. A soldier, no doubt under orders from his major, got behind the wheel and they set off up the road between abandoned houses.

But as they travelled the short distance back to the old convent, she thought about James and complications. About cracked skulls and meningitis and the myriad bacteria he might have picked up from the water he'd swallowed.

Should she on this occasion call in the helicopter herself? Get the lieutenant flown straight out to Vereton or wherever the army wanted him admitted?

CHAPTER EIGHT

KIRSTEN arrived back at the hospital to find that Lt Ross had not only been admitted, but was hooked up to a drip and was already breathing a high concentration of oxygen.

'Mary and I will X-ray him while you dry out,' Ken told Kirsten, who stood in the passage with muddy water pooling around her feet.

'I'll be right down,' she promised, and dashed into her room for clean clothes, then headed for the bathroom.

What she wanted was a long soak in a bath, or at least ten minutes thawing out under steaming hot water in the shower. What she got was a quick splash, in and out, time to wash her hair and remove the more obvious patches of sticky mud.

She knew Ken would have tested James's reflexes, would have used the Glasgow coma scale and the DERM mnemonic to assess his condition, but because it was James—or perhaps because it was a soldier—Kirsten was still anxious.

'There's a hairline lineal fracture, not displaced, on the temporal bone,' Ken told her, meeting her outside the room he'd allotted to James. 'I'd say that whatever hit him and caused the flesh wound either knocked him into something hard, or he was bounced against something as he was swept away.'

Ken's hesitancy told her there was more.

'What?' she asked.

'He's conscious, answering questions, responding to physical and oral stimuli. Pupils constricting to light, respiration good. He feels sick, which is natural considering

111

the amount of water he probably swallowed, but he can't remember anything about the accident—'

'That's not unusual,' Kirsten said.

'Or who he is,' Ken finished.

'Oh!'

They'd come to the crux of the matter.

'Temporal lobe injury can lead to temporary amnesia,' she reminded Ken. 'Hopefully, that's all it is.'

Again she considered complications.

'Any bleeding or loss of fluid from his ear?'

Ken shook his head, then qualified the gesture. 'Well, he was so wet, water was coming out everywhere, but since we dried him off and got him into clean clothes, there's been no sign. Mary's doing half-hourly obs—in fact, she's sitting with him as he's a bit disorientated still.'

'I'd better see him. Should we stitch the scalp wound?'

'I've taped it closed,' Ken told her. 'The water business worries me. We stitch it closed and there's some rare microbe hidden away in his tissues, we could get a wholesale infection.'

Kirsten agreed, but the problem of what to do with the soldier nagged at her as she went in and reintroduced herself to the young man.

Mary ducked away and Kirsten sensed she was glad to escape, something she understood when James Ross revealed a very fractious side to his nature.

'You must be able to give me something,' he complained. 'To help me remember things.'

'It will come back to you,' she told him, although no one could guarantee that it would—or when. 'Rest and relax, give it time. At the moment your body is more concerned with battling the germs you swallowed in your swim than restoring your memory. Once you've picked up again, it will come back.'

'I don't believe you!' he snapped at her. 'You doctors are all the same. Reassuring liars, the lot of you.'

'Perhaps you should have left him to drown,' a deep voice said, and Kirsten turned to find a still wet Harry behind her.

'I can always throw him back the way the fishermen do.' She looked at the puddle he was making on the floor. 'Shouldn't you be getting into dry clothes?' she asked, then smiled when she considered how often they'd had this conversation.

'When I've had a word with James here,' he said, his eyes returning her smile as if he understood exactly what she was thinking. He turned to his subordinate.

'Well, how are you feeling?'

James eyed him warily.

'The knock on his head has caused temporary amnesia,' Kirsten explained to the major. She then added to James, 'This is Major Harry Graham, the boss of your outfit. You usually call him sir.'

She saw James's hazel eyes darken with frustration and reached out to touch him on the shoulder.

'Don't force yourself. Relax. I'm sure the major would be happy to visit you later—when you've had a sleep—and tell you anything you need to know then.'

She gestured to Harry to leave the room, and followed him out, correctly anticipating his immediate reaction which was to turn to her and demand, in a whisper loud enough to echo down the passage, 'What's this amnesia thing? How badly hurt is he? Have you called the search and rescue helicopter? Alerted someone that we need him airlifted out?'

'Will you keep your voice down?' Kirsten snarled at him. 'In fact, come into my room where we can speak normally.'

She led the way.

'The floor's already wet where I dripped on it,' she told him when he hesitated in the doorway. 'If you stay off the carpet it won't be so bad.'

She found a clean towel and handed it to him. After rubbing it through his hair to stop the water trickling down his face, he dropped it on the floor and stood on it.

Well trained!

'He needs immediate attention,' he said, picking up where he'd left off in the passage. 'Experts. The army has doctors—and access to the best of civilian specialists.'

'No specialist on earth can restore his memory at this stage,' Kirsten told him bluntly. She took a turn around the room then faced him again, looking into the dark eyes as she tried to impress on him that she knew what she was doing. 'I'm sure it's simply post-traumatic amnesia—loss of memory following a blow to the head—and his memory will return. In my opinion it will return faster if he remains with people he knows and in the familiar environment of the platoon, even though you're not in your regular camp.'

She waited but when the major said nothing she added, 'Look. It's up to you. If you want him sent on, then I'm happy to do it. Heaven knows, we've enough on our plates with the waters about to arrive, without taking in extra patients.'

Harry frowned at her and Kirsten realised he didn't like the responsibility being thrust back on him. Which was strange because she'd judged him as very much a leader— a man who both accepted and enjoyed the responsibility for his men that was an integral part of his job.

'I don't know enough about it to make that decision,' he eventually complained. 'I don't have the medical knowledge.'

'Then phone someone who does,' she retorted. 'One of your experts. I'm the kind of doctor who welcomes a second opinion. I'm not going to get huffy because you don't want to take my word for it.'

He frowned at her for a moment, lifted his shoulders in an 'I don't know' kind of gesture, and hovered.

The hovering routine unsettled Kirsten. For a start it reminded her he was back in her room, and she didn't want recurring images of him there.

And he looked uncomfortable, which made her feel even worse as it prompted a desire to comfort him in some way, preferably a way that included putting her arms around him!

Not a good idea!

He broke the silence with a sneeze—breaking also the spell that had been tangling her thoughts and emotions.

'Go!' she said, pointing to the door. 'Get out of your wet clothes, make your phone call. Then don't you have a levee bank to rebuild, or are you going to allow the flood waters to find their own way through town?'

He stepped off the towel, bent to pick it up and handed it to her.

'I thought doctors were supposed to be overloaded with caring and compassion,' he complained. 'Offering solace and comfort rather than ultimatums and orders to go.'

She grinned at him.

'Not this doctor!' she said cheekily. 'Let me know what you decide about the lieutenant.'

Harry went, hurrying now. He didn't know why he'd been struck dumb, standing there on the towel in the middle of her room. Not that she wasn't right about him having plenty to do. He'd left his men struggling to fill the breach in the levee bank, which meant the work on raising the level at the upper end of town had been halted.

Then there was Lt Ross.

Kirsten's words about him staying with friends, in familiar surroundings, made sense, but what if the injury was worse than she realised? If he sent the man to town…

Thinking about Kirsten's words, it brought an image of her to his mind, and it was difficult to get past it and back to thoughts of James.

Get a second opinion, he said to himself. He'd phone the doctor, a mate of his, back at the field hospital at the base and get him to make enquiries—leave the decision up to him.

'What's she like, the doctor on the ground?' Major Paul Gamble asked Harry when they were finally connected.

About five-four, with brown curls and lively blue eyes, Harry's mind responded, but he managed to answer more sensibly than that, giving as his opinion that Kirsten was definitely dedicated and seemed very sensible.

'What she's suggested makes sense,' Gamble told him. 'But if you're worried, let me talk to her. I'll suggest she has a contingency plan should the lieutenant's condition deteriorate. In fact, I'm not doing much down here, with most of the company off fighting floods. I could get someone to drop me in and check on Ross myself.'

Harry knew he should have felt relief at the suggestion. If Gamble made the decision it let him off the hook. But the thought of Paul Gamble, legendary lover of the field hospital unit, staying, even temporarily, in close proximity to Kirsten McPherson didn't sit comfortably with him.

'I don't think that will be necessary,' he said firmly. 'And I'll speak to her about contingency plans.'

He sneezed as he hung up the phone and decided he'd shower first.

Kirsten visited her patients, finding Meg and Libby in with Cathy, and Anthony playing draughts with Chipper. It seemed her arrangement to keep the children in the attic rooms during the day was failing.

'No way! They help pass the time,' Cathy told her when

Kirsten asked if the children were a nuisance. 'I mean, it isn't as if we're all inundated with visitors. And the baby just eats and sleeps—he's totally boring. Now I'm up and about, I'd just as soon be sitting in with Brett as sitting here by myself.'

'Brett?' Kirsten echoed, then remembered it was Captain Woulfe's first name. She must be catching the major's habit of referring to them by their rank.

Cathy was telling her something else, about Brett's home town being not unlike Murrawarra, but she'd lost track because thinking about the major had triggered the memory of his strong arms wrapped around her body as they'd waited for the boat to return for them.

'I'd better check on James,' she said, firmly shifting her mental gears back to work.

He was sleeping quietly, and Mary, who came out of Chipper's room to report she was still doing obs, explained he'd drifted off almost as soon as the major had left the room.

'Perhaps just seeing him, even if he didn't know who it was, reassured him in some way,' she said, and Kirsten agreed it could be possible. She didn't know enough about amnesia to confirm it or deny it.

'Let me know if there's any change at all,' she told the nurse. 'A lung infection is a major worry when he's been immersed like that.'

Again she pondered sending him to town. Perhaps she shouldn't have dumped that decision on Harry's shoulders.

Uncertainty drove her back into James's room where she picked up his chart, before heading to her office. The good thing about country practice these days was the availability of experts on the end of a phone line. Bypassing Vereton, she phoned a neurologist she'd studied under years before. He was now a professor, conducting research into brain injuries, and universally acknowledged as a top man.

He wasn't in his rooms but an obliging secretary had him paged and he phoned back within in minutes.

Once politeness had been observed, she explained the situation, read out the results of the tests they'd conducted and asked for his opinion.

'I'm against moving head-injured patients on principle,' he told her. 'Unless there's need for further investigations—a scan, MRI, perhaps surgery. Your man doesn't sound too bad. In fact, if loss of memory is all he's suffering from—and a decent sort of headache, I'd assume— he's been lucky.'

'So keep him here?' Kirsten asked, wanting the decision unequivocal.

'Keep him there,' Charles Gresham told her. 'But continue obs and be prepared to go in if there's any sign of pressure building up inside his skull.'

'Thanks for bringing that up!' Kirsten said dryly, as the thought of having to drill a burr hole in James's skull made her shiver.

'Are you giving him antibiotics?' Charles asked. 'Prophylactically, it might be a good idea—get in before an infection starts.'

Kirsten, who'd considered it but had then set the option aside, talked this through with him and was convinced it would be advisable.

Much relieved, she thanked her former mentor and hung up. At least now she'd have some back-up if Harry moved into the attack again.

She returned to her patient who was still sleeping naturally. Rather than take the risk that he might be allergic to penicillin, she'd wait until he woke and she could speak to him about any reactions, although whether someone with amnesia would remember if he had allergies...

None that he knew of, was his eventual reply, but Kirsten decided to err on the side of caution. It was after eight and, although one detachment of the soldiers was still working under arc lights, she was fairly certain Harry would be in the building.

She tried the downstairs room he was using as an office first, but the orderly on duty there thought the major had retired for the night.

'Could you check for me?' she asked the young soldier. 'I wanted to ask you about your usual medical facilities. Do you have an army doctor or hospital unit back at your base?'

'Dr Gamble, that would be,' the young man said. 'I can put you through to him without bothering the major.'

Kirsten knew she should find this offer a relief, but even as she asked the soldier to go ahead and get the doctor she was conscious of slight disappointment.

This wouldn't do, she told herself sternly while she waited to be connected. The man's a virtual stranger, a career army officer who will be out of your life before you know it.

'Dr Gamble on the line, Doctor.'

She took the receiver and said a tentative hello, but the man's warm response banished any reticence and she was soon chatting to him as if they were old friends.

'You studied at Sydney University?' she said, impressed by his acceptance into the oldest medical school in the country.

The talk turned to professors they'd had, subjects they'd liked and loathed, and took a long time to get to the reason for her call.

'I'm assuming it's about Lt Ross. Harry phoned me earlier.'

Kirsten explained her dilemma.

'Look, I'm not in my office now, so I can't pull his medical records. You're quite right. Allergies will be recorded on them. OK with you if I call you back?'

Kirsten assured him it was more than OK. James's med-ical file might also contain information that could help her in this situation. Previous head injuries. A history of con-cussion.

She thanked the man and hung up, then realised she hadn't given him a number.

'He'll call back on this phone,' the orderly suggested. 'He'll have the number.'

'Do you mind me waiting here?' Kirsten asked, and the soldier smiled.

'No ma'am,' he assured her. 'I'm so bored I've been counting the stones in the wall. Usually on a detail like this there's filing to do, paperwork, that kind of thing, but out here there's not much except mind the phone. Communication lines must be kept open, it's the army's way.'

Kirsten asked him where he came from and they dis-cussed city versus country life.

'Would you like a cup of coffee, ma'am? We've good stuff here, and a proper pot to make it in because the major likes real coffee.'

Kirsten guessed this was a special favour and, feeling weary enough to fall asleep on the chair, agreed.

So she was sitting with her feet up on the major's table, a cup of his best Brazilian mocha in her hand, laughing at something Paul Gamble was saying on the phone, when Harry walked in.

She dropped her feet to the ground, shot upright in the chair, spilled coffee down her front, swore, then dropped the phone.

'You're wet again,' she said to the cause of her confu-sion.

'You're not so dry yourself,' he pointed out as she flapped her shirt to keep the heat away from her skin. 'Are you selling my coffee or giving it away, Corporal?'

Kirsten watched as the young man tried to disappear into the wall that had kept him occupied earlier.

'Someone on the phone?' Harry asked.

He lifted the fallen receiver and held it to his ear.

'Hello?'

Paul must have held on through the confusion, for Kirsten heard his deep voice greeting Harry, then a bit of conversation that sounded like, 'You sly old dog.'

It made no sense at all so, having, much earlier, found out what she needed to know, she thanked the hapless young man and, leaving him to bear the brunt of his superior's wrath, made a cowardly escape from the office.

James Ross had no listed allergies and had been given penicillin without ill effect when suffering a bout of tonsillitis. Paul Gamble agreed that some antibiotics dripping into him would be a good idea.

Kirsten and Joan were both kept busy overnight. Although not feverish, James was still restless and disorientated, and very, very irritable. And to further complicate matters, Brett Woulfe was finding the plaster uncomfortable.

'I don't think it's the plaster,' Kirsten said to Joan when they sat down together over a cup of tea at midnight. 'He seems to have a rash on his torso and forearms. If that's affecting the skin on his leg, no wonder he's uncomfortable.'

'Well, he's asleep now,' Joan told her, 'so why don't you go to bed? You can't keep up these twenty-four hour efforts for too long.'

Kirsten knew she was right, but James's condition and Brett's discomfort bothered her. And Moira was deteriorating and she had to make a decision about instituting tube feeding, something Moira was vehemently against.

'I'll do a quick walk around the patients first,' she said, 'then, yes, I'll go to bed.'

Mr Curtis was sleeping soundly—thank heavens his dementia hadn't yet led to wandering. Who knew where he'd end up in the flooded town? Chipper was groaning in his sleep, but that was normal. Cathy, with the baby in a crib beside her bed, was snoring gently, the baby's snuffly sounds like tiny echoes of the noise.

Brett, as Joan had told her, was out of it, no doubt exhausted after an uncomfortable afternoon. Mr Graham, propped on pillows to help him breathe, was dozing peacefully, and even James had finally succumbed to sleep.

She was heading back towards her bedroom when she heard a noise from the foyer and turned that way instead. The big entrance area was illuminated only by the light from the passage, so the form that crossed it was shadowy.

Kirsten swung her torch towards the figure and turned on the light, catching Harry in its beam. He was dry this time, and resplendent in pyjamas striped in royal blue and scarlet.

'Well, that's a splendid sight at midnight,' she joked, although her heart was jolting uneasily—no doubt because of fright, and nothing to do with a pyjama-clad major. 'Why are you lurking around the place?'

'I'm not lurking!' he responded. 'I was pacing.'

'Pacing? Is it a new form of exercise? I've heard of step exercise, but pacing sounds more like something horses do.'

'Pacing back and forth,' he said crossly. 'It helps me think.'

'At midnight?'

'I couldn't sleep, and would you mind turning off that light? You're behaving like a police interrogator out of a B-grade movie.'

Kirsten chuckled.

'You are in bad way, though I'm not surprised you couldn't sleep, with the noise those pyjamas must make.'

As her eyes adapted to less light, she saw him glance down at them.

'The pyjamas…' he muttered.

'Very loud,' she explained, then took pity on him. 'Do you want something to help you sleep?'

'No, I don't,' he snapped, and she held up her hands in surrender.

'Hey, I wasn't suggesting illicit drugs, just a mild sedative. Or a hot drink. That might help.'

'I don't want anything,' he said, then, apparently remembering his manners, added, 'Thank you.'

His tone was even more dismissive than his words, so Kirsten said goodnight and walked away. But the major's insomnia bothered her. Was he worrying about his two hospitalised soldiers? Was she making his job more difficult by keeping the men here?

She made a mental note to ask him in the morning and went to bed, sleeping deeply and dreamlessly until a knock on the door roused her at seven.

'I'm just going off duty,' Joan told her. 'Brett's rash is a lot worse. He says he had measles vaccine as a child but it could be rubella. His temp's slightly elevated, but apart from discomfort from the rash beneath the plaster there are no other symptoms.'

Kirsten thanked Joan, and as she dressed began to consider how they could get Brett up the stairs to the first floor. When the hospital board had decided to shift patients into the old convent, their renovations had included the installation of showers for patients on the ground floor. But upstairs, in the bathrooms used by the staff, were deep, old-fashioned baths.

She made her way out to the foyer and studied the stairs. The orderly on duty, a different soldier this morning, emerged from the temporary office and greeted her cheerily.

'How am I going to get a soldier with his leg in plaster up those stairs and into the bath?' she asked him, and he walked with her, apparently considering her problem, as she went up and along the passage, past the room she knew Harry used to the big bathroom.

'Getting him into the bath might be a problem,' the corporal told her, standing beside her while she mentally measured up the old claw-footed tub. 'Although I'm sure the major would lend you a couple of men to lift him in and out.'

They were standing side by side, considering the matter, when, like the nemesis he was becoming in Kirsten's life, the man himself appeared.

'Shifting the office to the bathroom, soldier?' he asked, causing the young man to leap about a foot in the air before embarking on a string of half-sentence excuses.

'He's helping me with a problem,' Kirsten explained, trying not to stare at the trim, first-thing-in-the-morning-and-still-dry Harry Graham. Although in fatigues again, he looked every bit a soldier, and something in his appearance, or perhaps his bearing, was so admirable she felt awkward in his presence. 'It's Captain Woulfe.'

Harry moved closer and peered into the bath.

'Lose him down the plughole, did you?' he asked, and Kirsten forgot about feeling awkward and responded to his banter with a grin.

'It's James we'd like to lose,' she countered, then relented. 'No, I don't mean that. And to get back to Captain Woulfe, he seems to have developed German measles now and the rash beneath the plaster is irritating him unbearably. I thought a bath—the plaster can get wet—with sodium bicarbonate to neutralise the rash's irritation. The corporal and I were working out how to get him up here.'

Harry looked at her for a moment then smiled.

'Considering the stairs, it would be far better if we could

take the bath to him. I'll talk to my CSM and see what the men can rig up in his room. You want all of him in this tub, or just his leg?'

'You can't do that. As well as a big enough container—and all of him should go into it—you need water and some-where for it to drain to when he's finished.'

He smiled at her disbelief.

'Just wait and see,' he said, then he turned to the orderly. 'Get the CSM up here for me, would you?'

The lad left the room so hastily that Kirsten realised he'd been embarrassed at being caught in there with her.

'Leave it to me,' Harry said. 'We'll either get it to him, or him up here.'

'But you've got more important things to do. You can't be taking men away from their flood work.'

His eyebrows lifted.

'I won't neglect your precious town,' he told her, 'but I'm also responsible for my men's well-being. There are always soldiers on duty here at the camp—they'll sort something out for Woulfe. I'll let you know.'

She was dismissed, as the corporal had been, so she left the room, walking slowly back down the stairs, wondering what it was about Harry that was so appealing to her senses and so unsettling to her mind.

Harry watched her walk away and sighed. What was it about the woman? Every time he turned around she was there—usually chatting up one of his juniors.

Well, perhaps not chatting up, but laughing and joking with the men in a way she never did with him. She was more likely to snap at him, or tell him to change his clothes, though why he cared about what she did or how she acted, he couldn't fathom.

It couldn't just be attraction, although her blue eyes, cheeky curls and pretty face were definitely worth a second look. Any man would find her attractive.

But finding someone attractive, and feeling churned up in his stomach every time he chanced upon her unexpectedly, were entirely different matters.

Perhaps it was the flood, the uncertainty of not knowing exactly when the worst would hit—or how bad that worst would be.

He was assuring himself that this was the reason for his unsettled state when the CSM arrived. Not to work out how to provide a bath for Captain Woulfe but to announce that a small chopper was just landing.

'Brass dropping in, I expect,' he added laconically.

'Great!' Harry muttered. 'Just what I need. A five-minute blow-through from some publicity-seeking brigadier.'

The CSM refrained from comment, but he followed Harry down the stairs and snapped some order at the orderly now back on duty in the office.

Presumably it would mean that refreshments would be offered to whoever had arrived, then, no doubt, a tour of the flood-ravaged town would be required.

'Harry, my old mate!' a cheery voice greeted him as he reached the door. 'Heard some transport was headed this way so I dropped in to check on your boys in person. Can't have the local medico rushed off her feet, caring for our men,' Paul Gamble added, flashing his woman-slayer smile at Harry as he held out his hand in greeting.

He was in uniform, not fatigues—in the full kit—knife-sharp creases in his khakis, and brass so shiny he glowed. Everyone knew women went for men in uniform, Harry remembered glumly.

'Are you the only person on the chopper? Our only guest?' he asked, knowing he should be pleased it wasn't someone who'd demand a guided tour.

'Just little old me and some supplies,' Paul told him. 'Now, come on, man, time's awasting. Where can I bunk down? And where's the...patients?'

Harry scowled at him. He'd heard that pause and knew Paul had been about to say 'woman'. After chatting to Kirsten for who knew how long on the phone last night, he'd wangled his way out here to check on her in person.

And there wasn't one damn thing Harry could do about it.

He summoned the orderly, directed him to show the major to a room upstairs, then take him through to the hospital wing.

'I've work to do. You'll find your way around easily enough,' he said to Paul.

He might not be able to prevent the two doctors meeting, but he was darned if he was going to hang around to watch Lothario in action.

CHAPTER NINE

KIRSTEN was in her room, asking herself why the major's abrupt dismissal should have bothered her, when there was a tap on the door.

'Come in,' she called, thinking Harry might have come to tell her what they'd decided for Brett.

It wasn't Harry but the young orderly, and with him a very smart-looking soldier who introduced himself as Paul Gamble.

Kirsten shook his hand and smiled at him, though fuming inwardly that Harry had seen fit to bring the army doctor all this way without consulting her.

'Have you come to take over the army patients?' she asked, and his eyes, a clear hazel, smiled into hers.

'Not at all,' he said. 'I've every confidence in your ability to treat a mild concussion and a broken leg, but it was a good excuse to get away from the base for a few days.'

His smile did nothing to detract from his good looks, and even as Kirsten registered that he was a very attractive man she wondered why he didn't affect her the way Harry Graham did.

Not that being affected by the major was going to save him from her wrath over this latest arrogant act of his! She quelled her anger and smiled at the newcomer.

'Come on, I'll show you around. Introduce you to the staff. You can even visit the army boys if you feel you should.'

Paul bowed and smiled again, then stood aside to allow her to precede him through the door.

'I suppose I should at least pretend to be working while

I'm here,' he teased as he came behind her as she tapped on Brett's door.

His hand brushed, perhaps accidentally, across her shoulder and Kirsten wondered if he might be flirting with her.

Heavens! Was it so long since someone had flirted with her that she'd forgotten what it was like?

She opened the door and went in, then stopped, bemused to find the bed shifted against the far wall and a canvas tub rigged up. It was full of water and a large immersion heater was hooked over the side, no doubt heating it to a pleasant temperature. Hoses led in and out through the window and Kirsten had to assume it would all work.

Someone in the place jumped to the major's commands!

She nodded to the two soldiers assisting Ken, and introduced Paul to the nurse.

'You going to drown him? Has he been that much of a nuisance?' Paul asked.

'He's covered in an irritating rash and the part under the plaster is driving him mad. I've got him on antihistamines but thought a neutralising bath might help.'

Paul had walked past her to the bed, and was shaking Brett's hand while Kirsten explained.

'Good idea,' the other doctor agreed. He spoke to the two soldiers who were handling the tub, advised them to listen to Ken's instructions when they prepared to lift the captain, then said, 'Well, he seems to be in good hands. Shall we move on?'

Kirsten glanced at Ken who nodded to show he had everything under control.

'As if we don't have enough water around the place,' she said as they walked out. 'Now we've got *en suite* baths!'

She took him across the passage to where James was not only awake but already giving Peggy—who, like all the staff, was taking on extra duties during the crisis—a hard time over what he saw as shortcomings in her bed-making ability.

'Not happy in the service, Lieutenant?' Paul asked, and James sprang to a straight sitting position and saluted.

'Well, at least he's remembering he's a soldier,' Kirsten said quietly.

Then she stood back, signalled to Peggy to slip away while the going was good and watched as Paul dropped his casual manner and introduced himself.

'Even a slight knock on the head can scramble your memory at times. I know it's useless telling you not to force it but, believe me, forcing it doesn't help. Only time will cure you. Let things come back gradually. I bet you remember more this morning than you did yesterday.'

James nodded.

'I can remember who I am, like my family's names— that kind of who I am. And somehow I know I'm a soldier, although I'm not sure what that means.'

'Quite a lot to you,' Paul told him. 'You're a damn fine soldier. Young to be a lieutenant, and going places. Just lately you've been chafing at the bit because you're doing more administrative work than active exercises, but you have to learn the office stuff as well.'

'I was in an office,' James said slowly, 'before I blacked out.'

'Not immediately before,' Kirsten told him, 'but you're getting closer.'

She looked at Paul.

'Perhaps you'd like to stay with him for a while. You know where my room is. Come there when you're done and I'll finish your guided tour.'

It meant she'd have time to check her other patients, perhaps sit down with Bella and have a quiet cup of tea while they discussed the practical side of how things were going.

*　*　*

Paul didn't reappear until around lunchtime, and she knew from Mary that he'd sat all morning with James, and had later spent a little time with Brett Woulfe.

'Sorry about that,' he said. 'But I felt James needed more reassurance than anything and talking generally about the army seems to have lessened his disorientation.'

'I'm glad someone's here with the time and knowledge to help him,' Kirsten told him. 'Now, do you want the tour or would you prefer to do your own thing?'

'Definitely the tour,' Paul said. 'One of the nurses told me the building's an old convent. I can't wait to see over the place and feel the vibes so many lovely virginal women must have left behind. The place should be reeking with frustrations.'

Kirsten smiled at his nonsense.

'The major tells me there's not a lot of difference between a nun's cell and an army tent,' she said, leading him out and down the passage so they could begin at the outer entrance to the west wing.

'And how did that conversation come up?' Paul asked, his mobile eyebrows repeating the question.

Kirsten shrugged.

'Who knows how any conversation comes up with the major?' she said, then, hoping to shift the doctor's attention from Harry, she pointed out the wide entrance, initially constructed so the nuns could walk in pairs without catching their voluminous robes on the archway.

'It's ideal from our point of view—wide enough to take a gurney with staff on either side, and no steps on this side, which is why we chose to use this wing.'

'But you won't stay here?' Paul said, astonishment colouring his voice. 'Surely you'll return to your regular hospital when the floods recede.'

Kirsten sighed. She really didn't want to go through all the business of hospital closure again.

'Why?' she asked. 'This building is available. It's above flood level, which means patients would never have to be evacuated again. The stone walls mean the building is cool in summer and warm in winter. There's an abundance of room, a huge kitchen, a dining room, offices and room for expansion if we want to incorporate hostel or nursing-home services.'

'But it's old!' he said. 'These days they're tearing down old hospitals all over the country and building new state-of-the-art structures.'

'Because the old ones have been hospitals for a long time. And generally they were wooden structures, impossible to clean efficiently. This building might be old, but it has no accumulation of bacteria. Admittedly, the rooms we use for operating have been renovated with the latest in stainless steel and aluminium, but the rest of the building is just fine as it is.'

She opened the door into the theatre to show him what she meant, then led him through the recovery room and into the little theatre she'd used as a labour room when Cathy had had the baby.

'Well, that's better than I'd expected to find hidden behind your stone walls,' Paul admitted. 'But what about patient care, with all the patients tucked away in individual rooms?'

'Come and see,' she invited. 'There are rooms large enough for two patients to share but so far we haven't bothered. After all, don't patients in private hospitals pay big money for individual rooms? Isn't it seen as a bonus?'

She took the visitor in to Chipper's room and introduced him. He was on his own, and complained that the army had stolen Anthony, his most regular visitor, from him.

Moira was next, and as Kirsten watched Paul speak to the frail woman, answering his own questions then waiting patiently for her slight physical movement to signal agreement or disagreement, she decided that, for all his charming, easy manner, he was probably a very good doctor.

'Will you have to tube-feed her soon?' he asked as they walked away.

'I think I'll have to,' Kirsten told him. 'I'm putting off the decision because I know she'll know it's the beginning of the end. She can still manage soft food spoon-fed to her.'

'That's labour-intensive,' Paul pointed out, and Kirsten smiled at him. 'And it takes time.'

'One thing we have at the moment is time,' she said. 'If it takes three hours to get each meal into her, it doesn't matter.'

'That's hospice stuff,' Paul argued, and Kirsten nodded.

'But isn't that what a hospital should be? A provider of services to everyone? Particularly in a country town which can't provide all the individual services. Come and meet Mr Curtis. In a city he'd be in a nursing home but in a town which at any one time might only have one or two people requiring that level of care, it's not financially viable to staff such a place. Here we can share staff, as well as facilities like the kitchen.'

Paul said nothing, but he greeted Mr Curtis cheerfully and again spoke to the man for a few minutes before Kirsten moved them on.

Cathy was feeding the baby and waved them in to admire young Robert.

'Rob should be in to see him by tomorrow or the next day,' she said, her eyes sparkling with excitement. 'Being on the northern side of town, the water will start going down first out our way. Once the peak is past, he can safely leave for a few hours.'

Paul duly admired the baby, but Kirsten could tell he was thinking about Cathy's words.

'It seems incredible—she's in here with a new baby, and

not so far away her husband is totally marooned by flood waters.'

'It's been a rough few months for the locals,' Kirsten agreed. 'Well, that's my lot. The east wing is much the same as this, only not renovated at all. Kitchen through this way.'

The tour went on, Kirsten introducing Bella and Mrs Mathers who'd decided she would help out in the kitchen. Right up to the attics where Meg and Libby were dressing the rabbits in dolls' clothes.

'Anthony's down at the motor pool,' Meg said with great authority. Then she turned to Paul and said, 'You're in the army. Why do they call it a pool when there's no water in it?'

'You might have tried to extricate me. Come up with an emergency or something,' he complained as Kirsten led the way down to the first floor where most of the staff had their temporary accommodation.

'I thought you managed quite well,' she said, still chuckling over his stumbling explanation of lots of things gathered in one place also being called a pool. 'This is where your virgins all resided,' she added, waving her hand towards the two corridors branching off from the landing.

'At the moment, it's hospital staff to the left and army to the right—bathrooms in both directions so don't go losing your way.'

He turned and looked into her eyes.

'As if I would. I saw the bed in your so-called ''office'' downstairs. The only place I'd lose my way would be down there.'

Kirsten felt a shiver feather down her spine as she recognised the flirtatious approach. She wasn't sure how to handle it so opted for a change of subject.

'You didn't meet Mr Graham. He was on the IPPB unit when we were down there.'

Paul's eyebrows rose.

'No comment?' he said, and she shook her head, doubly embarrassed because the flare of heat in her cheeks would undoubtedly have given her away.

Harry came through the front door and saw the couple standing at the top of the steps. His first reaction was a sinking feeling—he knew he hadn't wanted Paul Gamble here. But as he moved towards them something in the way Kirsten held herself betrayed that she was ill at ease and he grew annoyed, thinking his doctor friend might have upset her.

'Well, what do you think of your patients?' he asked Paul, hoping to remind him that he was here to care for them, not flirt with Kirsten.

'Ah, they're in excellent hands,' Paul replied, taking hold of one of Kirsten's hands as if to illustrate his point. 'Delightful hands,' he added, while Harry noticed she wasn't exactly pulling it away.

'So you're leaving?' Harry asked him.

Paul shrugged, then smiled.

'Can't!' he said with infuriating nonchalance. 'We're flooded in, remember. The bird that dropped me off flew straight back out.'

'I'm sure I could arrange something,' Harry told him, frowning at the way he still held Kirsten's hand.

Why didn't she remove it from his grasp? Surely she'd seen enough of Paul to know exactly what he was like? And what were they doing upstairs? Inspecting Paul's temporary quarters?

'Any time!' he added, then he turned away before he said something he might regret, heading for the office where he could vent some spleen by roaring at his clerk. There was sure to be something he'd done wrong.

Kirsten detached her hand from Paul's clasp. She should have done it earlier, but Harry's sudden arrival had thrown her off balance, then something in the way he'd glared at her had made her forget it was there.

'I'd better get back to work,' she said to Paul as she hurried down the stairs.

'Good grief! Don't tell me you're afraid of our Harry. Let me assure you, his bark is far, far worse than his bite. Gentle as a lamb, he is, under that gruff exterior.'

'I'm not frightened of anyone,' Kirsten said, but all the same she'd just as soon Harry hadn't seen her holding hands with Paul.

Not when she wanted his help with her master plan, she told herself when the thought jolted her into wondering why.

The rain had eased again as Harry watched his men place the final sandbags on the levee bank. It was mid-afternoon and teams had worked through the night to fill the breach near the main street. He was now confident he could divert the worst of the water around the town. True, the water level in the already flooded streets would rise, but the full force of the new surge should sweep past, saving the buildings that would otherwise be directly in its path.

There was nothing to do now but wait for the peak, expected tonight around midnight.

He dismissed his driver and made his way on foot, moving somewhat reluctantly back towards his temporary HQ. With everything under control, the volunteers having been sent home to rest and a few of his men keeping watch, he could take a break himself.

Or spend some time with Martin Graham, tell him what they'd done in preparation—maybe try to gauge a little of the man's personality—learn a little of his life.

The inner uncertainty that had kept him pacing in the night niggled at his stomach. If only he could talk it over with someone who knew the man—someone who also knew and understood the old man's frailty.

Someone like Kirsten McPherson.

He groaned to himself as he climbed the hill.

He'd already judged her to be a competent and caring physician, so why was he so reluctant to discuss his problem with her?

'Because you're afraid of revealing too much of yourself to the woman,' he heard himself reply aloud.

And avoided asking himself why because he already knew, and didn't fancy, the answer.

'Do you often talk to yourself?'

He blinked hard as the subject of his cogitations materialised in front of him.

'Did you levitate here?' he demanded, trying to still the rapid beating of his heart.

'No, I walked down in the normal way,' Kirsten told him, and he could hear a newly familiar gurgle of laughter beneath the words and see the merriment again in her sparkling eyes.

'You were so lost in your own thoughts you didn't see me,' she added in her kindly way.

He forced his gaze away from her sweetly pretty, portrait-painting face and pulled himself together.

'Were you looking for me?'

'Not really. Just getting some fresh air, checking on the flood level. Stretching my legs.'

Harry heard the list of explanations but the 'not really' right at the start had given him heart.

'Not really?' He repeated the words as a question.

She half turned, studied the waters for a moment, shrugged her shoulders, then spun back and raised her head so her eyes met his, a hint of defiance in the blue depths.

'You talked about strategic planning. I need a plan. At the moment we're reacting to each crisis as it occurs, rather than working our way steadily forward, and I wondered as you're here and know about strategies and stuff, if you'd—'

The flow of words ended as abruptly as they'd started but before Harry had time to make sense of them she launched into speech again.

'But, of course, it's not your concern, and not your business or your problem as you'll soon be gone from here and, anyway, planning to fight an enemy is probably very different from planning to fight a government department...'

Her voice trailed off and she looked so dejected he wanted to give her a good hug—though when he'd last felt the urge to hug someone he couldn't think!

'Is it so very bad, your hospital problem?' he asked, forgoing the hug but resting his hand on her shoulder in what he hoped she'd interpret as a comforting manner.

'Yes, it is!' she said stoutly, not moving out from under his hand which emboldened him to move his thumb against the soft white skin on her neck.

Comforting only, of course.

'The area manager's talking about cutting off our funds. Old Mr Graham, as chairman of the hospital board, did most of the negotiating—well, arguing really—with them, and now he's so ill I know I can't worry him with this latest blow. Jim Thompson's in hospital, and everyone else is either fighting the flood or evacuated so I have to come up with something myself.'

She had moved as she was speaking, not away from his hand but turning more towards him, so now, as well as imploring blue eyes, he had an all too close-up view of a pinkly soft and tantalising mouth.

And the only strategy he could bring to mind was one that involved seeing the blue eyes close as he bent to taste those tempting lips. He reminded himself that he was a soldier—on duty even—trained to resist diversions...

'Harry?'

The huskiness that caressed his name, the uncertainty in that softly murmured word, sent a shiver down his spine, and no amount of military training could withstand the purely primal urge to take this woman in his arms and kiss the breath out of her.

He slid his hand off her shoulder, down her back, feeling the bones beneath her flesh, the heat of that flesh beneath her clothes. Wanting to prolong the moment, put off the instant when their lips would meet, he drew her closer, his eyes locked on hers, seeing acceptance as well as questions, knowing she, too, felt the strands of attraction drawing them—

'Sir?'

Anthony's piping voice brought him stiffly to attention, his hand dropping off the doctor's back, allowing her to scurry a few paces backwards as if she, too, was as embarrassed by their closeness as he now was.

'Grandad wondered if you could visit him. When you're not busy, that is.'

The child's curious brown gaze shifted from Harry's face to Kirsten's then back again.

'Did Kirstie have something in her eye?' he asked, and Harry found himself smiling, although his body was strung as tight as fencing wire and he fancied Dr McPherson was feeling much the same way.

'We thought so,' he temporised, thinking of the desire he'd thought he'd seen before those dark lashes had fluttered down, just as he'd imagined they would. 'I'm not busy now. I'll come up and see your grandad.'

Kirsten nodded in answer to the question in Harry's eyes then sighed as he turned away from her. She watched Anthony slip his hand into his new friend's larger one, and sighed again as the pair walked off up the hill.

And what's this sighing business? the last skerrick of common sense left in her brain demanded. You should be glad Anthony arrived when he did. Harry Graham was off limits. He's passing through, here today and gone next month. And no matter how seductive his brown eyes, how firm the feel of his fingers on your skin, unless you want to get your heart broken you'll steer clear of him.

She stared out across the flooded town and sighed again. Then nodded. The voice of common sense had been right. She was committed to Murrawarra, at least for the foreseeable future while she fought for the hospital's survival. And Harry was regular army. He would be ordered out of her life before long, no matter what sparks of attraction might have unexpectedly sprung up between them.

Added to which, the attraction itself was weird—totally out of whack—when she considered how aggravating she found him. That morning she'd been furious with him for bringing Paul Gamble to town and only the thought of seeking his help over 'the plan' had made her decide to set that little matter aside for the moment.

How could she possibly be attracted to such an infuriating, domineering man?

'Are you going up, staying put or walking down?'

Paul's question brought her out of her gloomy reverie and she turned to smile at him.

'Walking down to see where it's reached,' she told him. 'How much have you seen?'

He fell in beside her.

'From the air it looked like an ocean of murky brown water—stretching as far as one could see. It seemed impossible to believe anything could be left standing in its wake, but when we landed I saw the tops of buildings and realised that, beneath it all, the town still stood.'

They talked about the previous floods and Kirsten pointed out the various landmarks now all but obliterated by the water.

'This can't have been the first time it's happened,' Paul

said, 'so why wouldn't the town have been moved, perhaps a century ago, when the locals realised it was in the path of flood waters?'

Kirsten shrugged.

'Most floods leave it a little damp around the edges. The flood-prone houses and businesses all have their routines for preparing for the water, and then dealing with the mess. And if you're ever here in winter you'll realise just how cold it gets on the hills when the westerly winds whistle across the continent and batter at any building foolish enough not to seek the shelter of the valleys.'

She turned because the sight depressed her, and began to walk back up the hill, answering Paul's questions but wishing it was Harry with her—in spite of the fact she wasn't interested in Harry.

Forgetting she was annoyed with him.

Maybe the brown eyes—

'I met your Mrs Mathers earlier,' Paul interrupted her thoughts as they walked back into the hospital wing. 'From what she told me, she's one of those who are used to floods.' He turned to Kirsten and smiled. 'Did she really have all her jewellery stolen in the last flood?'

Kirsten grinned at him.

'Trying to imagine what "jewellery" she might have had?'

Paul nodded.

'Not that anything would surprise me,' he assured Kirsten, who chuckled at this patent lie.

'It was a bead curtain,' she explained. 'The kind people hang across an open door to deter the flies. Multicoloured beads in blue and scarlet and green that shone like jewels in the sunlight.'

'Jewels!' Paul gasped, laughing so hard he could barely speak. 'Of course! She even told me what they were. Emeralds and sapphires and rubies.'

'They meant a lot to Mrs Mathers,' Kirsten told him, although she was enjoying sharing the light-hearted moment with him. Until the door opened opposite where they stood and Harry stepped out, the scowl on his face stealing the laughter from her lips.

'Perhaps you could enjoy your joke somewhere else,' he said in quiet but steely tones. 'Mr Graham is just dropping off to sleep and this is supposed to be a hospital.'

Paul looked from him to Kirsten, raised one eyebrow and murmured, 'Touchy!' Then he disappeared in the direction of Brett Woulfe's room.

'I'm free if you wish to discuss strategy,' Harry said to Kirsten, but so coldly she decided the last thing she wanted was to spend more time in his company when he was in this mood.

But could she knock back his offer? Look a gift horse— or gift infantry, in Harry's case—in the mouth?

'We can talk in my room,' she said, and, her heart heavy with uncertainty, she turned and led the way.

But once they'd reached her office and she'd shut the door so they could discuss the matter in peace, waving Harry into a chair, it seemed he was more anxious to discuss the patient he'd just left than the hospital's dilemma.

'I'm afraid my visit might have tired him,' he said, no sooner settled in the chair than he was out of it to pace the room again. 'I did the talking at first, told him what we'd done as far as the levees were concerned and how we hoped to send the main surge around the town instead of through it, but then it seemed he wanted to talk about the hospital…'

Harry paused in his pacing and turned to look at the doctor, sitting so still beside her desk she might have been a statue.

Portraits—statues—he shook his head to clear it of ridiculous fantasies.

'Well, aren't you going to say something?' he demanded when she continued to sit there, frowning at him.

'What do you want me to say?' she asked. 'Do you want reassurance you haven't tired him when you're intelligent enough to know that talking is an effort for him?'

She tilted her head a little to one side, and her frown grew more perplexed.

'Besides, I don't think that's what's bothering you at all. I know you've an empathy with the old man, but...'

Kirsten left the sentence incomplete but indecision held Harry back from telling her what was really troubling him. He couldn't bear for her to feel bad towards him if he eventually decided there was nothing to be gained by making himself known to Martin Graham.

And he couldn't *do* that if he felt his admission of who he was, and what had happened thirty-two years ago, would cause more grief and pain to the old man and possibly put his health in further jeopardy. He did what any sensible man would do and changed the subject.

'This plan of yours. You've got to use people power— voting power. Get someone who might conceivably lose his seat—or win the seat—in the next election on your side. That's one strand of your strategic plan. Mr Graham tells me you've already got a petition going, but to get the numbers to influence government you need to draw more attention to the problem, need a wider campaign. Media is good. Aim for airing the problem on one of those current affairs shows, and have another group of people willing to ring a couple of popular radio personalities on their phone-in sessions.'

Kirsten heard the words and knew she should be writing down these ideas but her heart was troubling her.

Because she knew instinctively that Harry Graham was using his rush of words, his rapid-fire suggestions, to paper over something else, something too painful for him to share.

Share with her.

And why should he? the scrap of common sense demanded.

Because I want him to, her unhappy heart replied.

CHAPTER TEN

'ARE you listening to me?'

The irritable demand brought Kirsten back to the present.

'Media, go on talk shows, get people beyond the district around Murrawarra interested in our plight. Yes, I've made a note of it all.'

She realised how patently untrue that was and added, 'A mental note.'

'You'll have the media opportunities when the flood goes through and the television reporters fly in to get graphic pictures of the aftermath,' Harry pointed out, but his voice was less forceful—softer—as if he was saying the words but thinking something else.

Her skin tingled as she remembered another 'something else'. Earlier in the afternoon—before Anthony had arrived.

Had he been about to kiss her?

An exasperated noise brought her to her senses.

'Women!' he muttered, striding back and forth across her square of carpet. 'It's like trying to figure nuclear fission. In fact, nuclear fission might be easier. One minute she wants a plan—a grand campaign—and the next she's sitting dewy-eyed at her desk, gazing into space and thinking who knows what!'

He stopped in front of her and frowned down at her.

'It's Paul Gamble, I suppose.' He growled the words with a fierce intensity. 'Well, let me tell you, the man is as well known for his inconstancy as he is for his womanising. Oh, he's charming all right, and as smooth as silk, but if you're expecting any long-term relationship, forget it, pretty doctor. He's a strictly love-'em-and-leave-'em type of man.'

His tirade brought Kirsten out of her dream of brown eyes and kisses. It also reminded her of a grievance she'd been almost willing to forget.

She straightened in her chair and glared up at him, hoping her eyes conveyed some of the anger she was feeling.

'Let's leave Paul Gamble's charm out of this conversation—though I wouldn't have thought someone like you would recognise charm if it bit you on the backside. Let's talk about you bringing him here—your lack of trust in my ability, your total disregard for my feelings when you asked your own doctor to fly in to take over my job.'

The escalating rage pushed her to her feet so she stood toe to toe—almost nose to nose—with this man whom destiny had thrust into her path, apparently for the sole purpose of adding to her multitude of problems.

'Second opinions are all very well, but to actually…' Kirsten prodded her finger into Harry's chest to emphasise her point, but before she could continue he captured it and then grasped her whole hand, his touch drying her lips, her mouth, so badly that no more words would come.

The brown eyes that had so enticed her stared down into hers, unreadable for a moment, then softening in a way that made the quivers start right up again.

'Paul Gamble came of his own free will,' Harry told her, his voice gruff now, not fierce at all. 'Do you think I'd want a snake like him around—?'

He stopped abruptly, uncertainty dimming the fire she'd seen flaring to life in the brown depths.

He dropped her hand and moved away, crossing to her window and looking out.

'I'm a soldier. It's my life. I'm moving on. You do see that, don't you?'

She did see that, more was the pity! She also understood.

There didn't seem to be anything she could say so she remained silent, staring at his straight, strong back—thinking how contrary attraction could be.

The tension in the room was growing, though it was nothing compared to the tightness in Kirsten's chest. She had to break it—make out that she didn't care.

Or, better still, that she didn't understand?

She drew a deep breath, blew it out, took another, then crossed to stand beside him, looking past the tents to where the water was noticeably higher.

'So you can't help me save the hospital,' she said, and inwardly congratulated herself on the evenness of her voice. 'Well, that's OK. You've given me some ideas. We've managed so far on our own. I guess we can keep going.'

He turned to her, his confusion so apparent she couldn't hide the smile that twitched across her lips.

There was silence for a moment, then he met and matched her smile with a teasing, slightly lopsided one of his own.

'You little witch!' he murmured, then he took her in his arms, bent his head towards her and kissed her firmly on the lips.

It was a mess, Harry realised as soon as he tasted the tempting sweetness. A snafu of major proportions, he thought as his tongue teased them into parting and warm moistness overwhelmed his senses.

Her slight body seemed made to fit against him, to mould its pliancy to the planes and angles of his drill-toughened bone and muscle. His fingers combed their way through her soft curls to hold her head steady as he drank in the nectar of her kisses and met the sudden heat of her response with even hotter demands of his own.

It's just a kiss, he told himself, struggling to breathe without lessening his assault or diminishing her response.

But his body knew it wasn't 'just' anything! It strained

against her melting softness, wanting to take more, give more, demand from her the ultimate acquiescence—the total submission that in the giving was also total domination.

'It's just a kiss!'

He heard the whispered echo of his thoughts—fortunately only part of his thoughts—as small hands pushed against his chest and a coolness on his lips told him she'd moved away.

Harry looked down at her downcast head, and saw the hectic flush on her cheeks. It didn't take a genius to work out she'd spoken to herself. He guessed it meant she was as rattled as he was. Which was some satisfaction!

'I have to see my patients,' she muttered, stepping backwards as if she needed to make space between them. 'You came from Mr Graham. He was asleep? Was that what you said?'

He guessed her stumbling sentences were an attempt at normality—and could hardly fault them as she was doing better than he was.

'He's asleep,' he managed to confirm. 'Or was when I left him.'

He paused, hesitating, wanting more than anything to confide in her—to ask her advice, seek her guidance.

'Kirsten?'

She looked up at him and the blueness of her eyes took his breath away. He forgot his problems, forgot the first kiss had been a mistake, and drew her back into his arms and began all over again.

Instead of pushing at his chest, this time her hands moved against it, then her arms slid around his waist and she was holding him as tightly as he held her, their bodies swapping sensations for which there were no words.

A sharp rapping on the door brought Kirsten to her senses and she broke away, pressing her fingers to her cheeks and scurrying towards her desk and dropping into her chair as she called, 'Come in.'

Ken stepped cautiously through the door and glanced from her to Harry.

'The army doctor's been looking for the major,' he said. 'And Allan Smith's just come in with a lump in his groin. Says it's been there for a while but he's been too busy to do anything about it until the major sent them home to rest today.'

She watched Harry slip away and felt a mix of relief and disappointment, though perhaps, with him out of the room, it would be easier to regain control.

'I'll come now,' she told Ken. 'Did you check for an infected wound?'

He grinned at her.

'What do *you* think?' he teased her. 'Apparently, he spiked his calf on something a week or so ago and then forgot about it. It's been a bit sore but those blokes have been too busy to worry about even basic first aid. The area is red, hot and tender to the touch but there's no outward indication of an abscess.'

Kirsten eased herself to her feet, pleased to have a problem of sufficient interest to take her mind off Harry Graham. But as she walked down the corridor to their newly set up A and E rooms, she realised Allan had presented her with more than an interesting problem—he'd brought a dilemma along with him.

He was sitting on one of their examination tables, his legs outstretched in front of him, looking supremely uncomfortable in this alien environment. Kirsten greeted him, then examined the black mark where something had pierced his skin and left behind who knew what bacteria before the skin had closed over again, trapping the bugs inside.

'There's obviously an infection there somewhere and I'm going to have to cut the skin and drain it out,' she told the man, who was one of the stalwarts of the local branch of the State Emergency Service. 'After that, I'll leave a plug of material in there to keep the wound open and allow any further infection to drain out.'

She eyed the grey-haired man warily.

'Is that suggesting anything to you?'

He studied her for a moment, then smiled.

'Can't you give me something—some antibiotics to fight the infection—and leave the leg as it is?'

Kirsten shook her head.

'The infection has already spread to your lymph glands—that's why you've got a lump in your groin. If I don't get rid of it, it will go on from there through your entire body and you'll be a very sick man.'

'But if you leave it open and I go back into the water...' He swung around, dropped his legs back over the edge of the table and was about to get off, obviously intending to leave his wound untreated if it meant he could no longer be part of the fight against the floods.

'Exactly,' Kirsten told him, holding up a hand in a 'wait right there' gesture. 'Listen. Most of the hard work is done. All you and your men can do now is wait for the water to go down, then help with the clean-up. I'm not saying that's going to be easy, but it's not as urgent. Surely there's a job you can do that doesn't involve wading around in bacteria-ridden slush.'

He looked at her, shook his head, scratched his fingers through his hair for a long minute, then finally nodded.

'I guess I could take over the roster from Bertie,' he suggested doubtfully. 'He's anxious to get into Vereton to see his missus and kids as soon as the back road's clear again. With the army here, one man won't be missed.'

'Excellent idea!' Kirsten told him. 'And the drain will only need to be in your leg for forty-eight hours at the most. After that I should be able to wrap the wound in a waterproof dressing, so if you do happen to get it wet it won't matter quite as much. But that doesn't mean plunging back into the thick of things again. At least, not until your leg's healed.'

She turned to Ken and together they stepped away.

'I think the area's too inflamed for a local anaesthetic to be effective when I do the incision. It's the pressure of the build-up of pus that causes a lot of the pain and to add extra fluid makes things worse.'

'A light anaesthetic?' Ken asked. 'I've checked his BP and pulse, and his records from previous visits don't list any allergies. What do you want?'

'Meperidine. One hundred grams IM, then a slow IV infusion of diazepam. It should make him drowsy enough to not worry about what we do. Meperidine first—it takes about twenty minutes to become effective.'

Ken moved away to prepare the injection and Kirsten explained to her patient what she intended doing.

'You're going to knock me out for a little cut on the leg?' Allan objected.

'Believe me, it's better this way,' Kirsten assured him. 'Now lie back and relax. The first injection is feel-good stuff. Ken will keep you company while it works and I'll do a quick check on the other folk we have in here and be back to do the cruel part.'

'You're all the same, you women,' Allan grumbled good-naturedly. 'Love inflicting pain on men.'

'Huh!' Kirsten retorted. 'What about the pain men inflict on women? I don't see many guys lining up to have the babies!'

'If that were only possible! Physically possible, I mean,' a deep voice said, and Kirsten turned to see Paul walking into the room, and behind him, looking cool, casual, and totally unconcerned, Harry.

'I'm taking Harry on the guided tour. Apparently you've

been too busy with other things to show him around. He was quite affronted when he realised I knew far more about the place than he did!'

Kirsten avoided checking to see Harry's affronted look. In fact, she rather hoped that Paul, in his role of tour guide, would move on to somewhere else.

Anywhere else.

'You going to introduce us to your patient?' Paul asked.

So much for hope, Kirsten thought as she did the right thing by all three men.

Harry, apparently recognising Allan from their joint efforts at the levee bank, showed no interest in his reason for being at the hospital and began instead to question him about likely weaknesses in the water-diversion plan. Ken returned as the conversation moved on to how best to organize the clean-up, the number of men that should be included in each crew and what equipment, apart from pumps and shovels, would be needed.

'Last time we didn't have enough pressure hoses. I know it sounds daft, using water where there's already been so much, but that shifts the mud faster than anything else,' Allan explained.

He looked at Harry.

'Your lot has plenty of that gear, then?' he asked, and as Harry began detailing what his 'lot' had brought with them Kirsten dithered.

What she should be doing was shooting the meperidine into one of Allan's muscles, but getting close to Allan to do that meant getting closer to Harry Graham.

Not advisable at this stage.

Or she could leave it all to Ken. Come back when Allan was ready for her scalpel.

Ken set the tray down beside the examination table and she stepped warily towards it. If only Harry had been on the other side…

'Want us out of the way?' Paul asked, and she flashed him a look of gratitude, then realised she might have overdone it somewhat when Paul winked at her and Harry, who'd been in a position to see both the smile and the wink, growled something unintelligible in her ear.

'Please!' she begged. 'Surely there's somewhere else the major hasn't seen.'

'The virgins' cells?' Paul suggested. 'Knowing Harry, it's probably been a while.'

Apparently it was a male joke, for Allan, Ken and Paul all laughed while Harry did his growling thing again and Kirsten felt acutely uncomfortable.

The two men left the room and she proceeded with her task, swabbing Allan's arm then easing the narcotic into the muscle.

'I'll be back,' she said to Ken, and left the room. What she needed was some breathing space, and now that her office held memories she didn't immediately want to face, the great outdoors would have been first choice. But she had patients to visit, staff to see. And the great outdoors were exceedingly damp.

Experience told her that if she didn't do a round now, things would almost certainly get hectic later. And fate being what it was, she'd regret she'd missed the opportunity.

She started with James, delighted when he smiled at her, his grumpiness lessening as he pieced his memory back together.

'Major Graham says it was you who pulled me out of the water,' the young man began.

'Biggest fish I've caught in ages,' Kirsten joked, but even the mention of Harry's name was starting the quivers now. She had to fight whatever it was between them. Think of something else.

'I thought about giving you a kiss and tossing you back,

the way the fisherman on TV does it,' she added lightly, 'but you looked good enough to keep.'

'I've seen that chap on TV,' James told her. 'I'm better, aren't I, if I can remember things like that?'

'Almost better, but you're to stay right there in bed and rest. I've been far more worried about the crack in your skull than your memory. I was pretty sure it would come back, given time.'

'But I can't remember hitting my head—or even being down near the levee bank. Major Graham's had me office-bound practically the whole time we've been in town.'

James sounded irritated again but, then, Kirsten knew how irritating Harry Graham could be. Which made the attraction thing even more peculiar.

Work, she reminded herself.

'You might never remember the few minutes prior to the injury,' she told James. 'That can happen with a blow to the temporal region of the brain. Don't let it worry you.'

James pulled a face that told her he didn't think much of losing even so small a piece of memory, but relaxed back against his pillows and didn't argue.

Kirsten chatted to him for a few minutes, repeated her instructions about rest, then moved on to visit Moira.

'She's been eating far better,' Peggy told her after she'd waved Kirsten back out into the corridor because Moira was sleeping. 'I thought we'd have to talk about tube-feeding, like you'd said, but today she's been really good.'

Kirsten heard the hope in the older woman's voice.

'If sheer will-power can keep someone alive, then yours is doing that for Moira,' she said huskily. 'You've been a fine friend to her, Peggy. A wonderful support.'

'She's so good it's easy,' Peggy whispered, her voice thick with emotions she rarely showed. Then she sniffed, and grinned at Kirsten. 'Well, I can't be standing here being maudlin, now can I? Bella will be needing a hand with the dinners.'

She scurried away and Kirsten smiled as she watched her disappear down the corridor.

Male voices from Chipper's room suggested that the major's guided tour had stalled again. Without conscious effort, Kirsten sorted out one voice in particular, reminded herself again how impossible it was and moved on, skipping her old friend to look in on Mr Curtis. Mrs Mathers was there, regaling him with the story of her rescue. True to his gentlemanly nature, the old man nodded and smiled, although Kirsten guessed the tale made little sense to him.

Harry had that gentlemanly streak in him—though whether learnt or natural, Kirsten didn't know.

And probably never would, she thought gloomily as she pressed on with her self-appointed task.

Next was Captain Woulfe, who was apparently comfortable enough after his bath, for he was engaged in a deadly game of Snakes and Ladders with Meg and Anthony.

'Don't let them bug you,' she warned the young soldier.

'Bug me? They're saving me from going right off my head with boredom. When can I walk on this cast?'

'Not for a while,' Kirsten told him, 'but we've wheelchairs available if you want to get around, although you'll be restricted to the building. I don't want you losing control and flying down the hill into the flood waters.'

Which will peak tonight and then go down, the town will be almost back to normal in a couple of weeks—and the army gone within the month!

Kirsten sighed as she pushed open the next door. This sighing business was becoming a habit. Best she stop right now!

Peter Phelps's room was empty and Kirsten guessed some army task had him up and about. She moved on. Cathy's room was also empty, but as a protesting cry echoed from the bathroom at that moment Kirsten headed that way.

'We're giving Robert his bath,' Libby told her proudly. She was standing on a small stool beside the low bench while Cathy held the squirming infant in shallow water in a small baby bath. Merryll hovered behind them, the official hospital presence that regulations demanded.

'So I see,' Kirsten responded. She'd checked young Robert herself earlier in the day and had found him remarkably healthy for someone who'd been unwittingly involved in flood rescue work for weeks before his birth.

But although she smiled, and made the right noises, the baby wasn't providing her with the usual joy she felt in the presence of a new life. If anything, it was making her feel depressed, making her wonder if her own life was lacking something.

'I'll be in A and E if anyone's looking for me,' she told Merryll.

At least as she lanced and drained Allan's abscess there'd be nothing to distract her or tempt her thoughts to stray.

But the operation was over in a matter of minutes, a plug of gauze inserted as a drain, the wound covered and Allan awake enough to be sent home, although Ken suggested he go through to the kitchen where Bella could probably be persuaded to give him an early dinner.

'It'll be better grub than we've been getting on the other hill,' Allan said. 'Next flood we're keeping one of the women here to cook for us. Jim Thompson appointed himself chief cook and he was hopeless, but Ernie took over when Jim went to town, and he's worse.'

The good-natured grumble reminded Kirsten why she liked country towns—and this country town in particular. People didn't ask for much, and were appreciative of what they had. They had an acceptance of life as it was, perhaps learned from years of living with the vagaries of nature.

And what some might have seen as a lack of ambition was, for most folk, simple contentment.

She said goodbye to Allan and waved Ken away.

'You take him through to the kitchen. I'll clean up here.'

She wasn't actually hiding, she told herself. Just seeking somewhere she could think in peace. With so few people in town, it was unlikely there'd be a rush of patients through A and E.

But how could you think through something that didn't exist? she wondered as she sealed the container of contaminated materials and tidied up the discarded packaging. Logic doesn't work on nothingness—can't grasp at quivers of response or a shift of something not yet understood, too deep inside her to be examined closely.

'It's like a mild infection—it will pass.' She said the words aloud in the hope they might be more emphatic that way.

'Now it's you talking to yourself,' a familiar voice said, and the sudden jolt along Kirsten's nerves made a lie of her valiant statement.

One glance at Harry's face told her he hadn't come to dally.

'There's a problem?' She moved automatically towards him then stopped, deciding distance was a wiser option.

'No.' His assurance came quickly, to be followed by an explanation that didn't quite gel. 'The water's rising faster than we expected. I'll see the men are fed and then we'll be on duty. Probably busy for a day or two. I—'

Came to say goodbye?

'Thought I'd let you know,' he finished, dashing the silly surge of hope or happiness Kirsten had experienced.

'All the best with it,' she said, deciding two could play this 'chance-met colleagues' game. 'And although no one's here to overwhelm you with thanks, I hope you know how much the town appreciates what the army is doing for it.'

His smile brought more than a quiver this time, but Kirsten quickly quelled the undesirable reaction.

'Why, thank you, ma'am,' he said, with a funny little bow. 'Especially as I know how hard it must have been for *you* to say those formal words of gratitude.'

Smile-generated tremors gave way to indignation.

'Oh, get out of here! Go fight the flood,' Kirsten told him crossly. 'You really are the most provoking man, Harry Graham. I try to be polite and what do you do? Mock me, that's what! We are—even I am—grateful, but if you don't want thanks then that's OK.'

Harry seemed taken aback—even hesitant—and said, 'Yes, well…' He let the end of the sentence vanish into the ether.

Kirsten found the urge to hug him had returned, although she knew full well that hugging Harry Graham would be dangerous.

'I'll try to keep in touch,' he said, and the return of strength to his voice, as well as the new stiffness in his bearing, told her he'd overcome whatever uncertainty he'd experienced and was once again back in full control.

'Good luck,' Kirsten said, then, her heart pounding from the onslaught of too many mixed emotions, she added, 'Stay safe.'

Harry nodded, as if that was what he intended doing, then he about-turned in a sharp, military manner and all but marched from the room, returning only seconds later to snap, 'And you stay safe as well. Keep away from the water. No foolish heroics. Hear me?'

Kirsten flipped a salute at his disappearing back and smiled into the now empty room, unable to ignore the tiny glow of happiness his words had lit inside her.

CHAPTER ELEVEN

THE next three days were hectic for the men protecting the town. With things slack at the hospital, Kirsten conferred with the mess sergeant and organised Bella to provide cakes and biscuits for morning and afternoon tea for the soldiers and volunteers working in the town. The army had the other meals more than adequately covered, their field kitchen a constant source of wonder to the hospital staff who made regular sorties down to town to check on what was happening.

'They're having beef stew tonight,' Peggy reported one afternoon. 'You wonder they can carry all the food they do.'

Kirsten pretended to be interested, but unless someone mentioned seeing Harry the reports seemed dull. What was one more wall of water anyway?

She'd caught glimpses of him from time to time—a wet figure dashing up the stairs—a dry figure dashing out of the front door—but knew from what she'd gleaned that he'd remained on duty throughout the worst of the inundation.

Paul Gamble had departed, airlifted out with Brett Woulfe when a medical helicopter had been freed from rescue operations further north. Kirsten had conferred with Paul and decided it would be better for Brett to convalesce where physiotherapy was available.

Following closely behind the peak of the flood came the press, their news helicopters as irritating as the gnats that swarmed above the water.

'I put up with them the first day,' Kirsten complained to

Ken when two had landed within half an hour, so close to the old convent that the building had reverberated with the noise, 'because I thought I might be able to interest them in the plight of the hospital. But, no, all they want are pictures of dead cows and ruined buildings, photographic evidence the town's been wrecked. It's all so negative!'

'It's human nature to take more notice of disaster than of triumph,' Ken reminded her. 'You only have to look at the lead stories on the evening television news. The viewers must love death and destruction.'

'I'll give them death and destruction!' Kirsten muttered as a whirring noise told her one of the helicopters was taking off. 'And I'll stop their little games.'

She stormed outside, where she found a camera-lugging young man running towards the remaining helicopter, whose whirring blades suggested an imminent departure.

'Hey, you!' she yelled above the clatter of the engine. 'Wait.'

The man glanced towards her, and hesitated long enough for her to get close.

'I want to talk to you!' she said.

He pointed towards the machine and shrugged and would have continued moving if she hadn't grabbed his arm.

'This is a hospital!' she told him. 'I have patients in there. I don't want your machines just landing and taking off whenever they feel like it. You tell the others.'

'Might as well tell that water down there to stop flowing,' he said cheerfully. 'Slow news week overseas, so we're using more of the flood than we normally would. And the army always makes good copy!'

On that note he departed, racing towards the helicopter which rose as soon as he was through the hatch-like door. But as the machine swung over the convent, he leaned out, camera pointed downwards, and Kirsten was reasonably certain her furious face and futilely waving fist would also feature on the evening news that night.

'Cut-away shot of the local doctor losing her cool?'

She spun around, coming face to face with Harry—more damp than really wet this time.

'It's all your fault!' she told him bitterly. 'Are they interested in my hospital? Oh, no, not when the army makes good copy!' She mimicked the reporters words.

'If you had any decency at all you'd have organised a war somewhere overseas this week. That way Murrawarra's floods wouldn't have attracted any attention at all.'

'I thought you wanted attention,' Harry said mildly, and Kirsten had to clench her hands into fists to stop herself strangling him.

'I want them stopped!' she told him. 'Can't you issue orders? Tell them not to come!'

'Telling the press not to go somewhere is like issuing an invitation to people to help themselves to some free money. They immediately assume there's something noteworthy happening and you get more of them, not less.'

He half smiled and Kirsten had to remind herself that she was angry and in order to stay that way half-smiles should definitely be ignored.

'Besides, the army's not allowed to order civilians around. Only other civilians can do that.'

Because of the effort of ignoring half-smiles, it took a minute to absorb what he was saying, but only a second or two for her anger to re-ignite.

'That didn't seem to stop you ordering me around when you first arrived.' She stepped closer and jabbed her finger in his chest. 'Telling me you were going to evacuate us by force!'

The half-smile grew into a full one, which took a lot more inner fortitude to resist.

'It was a bluff,' Harry admitted, thinking how attractive

he found her when she was cross and wondering if perhaps that showed an aberration in his character.

'Well, I'm not bluffing,' she said stoutly, 'and if you're not going to do anything to keep those helicopters away from my hospital I'll do it myself.'

'By waving your fist at them?' Harry teased. It was the way her eyes blazed that really got to him.

'By shifting my car!' she snapped, and then she whirled away before he had time to process the words, let alone work out what they might mean.

He discovered later, when he'd snatched a couple of hours' sleep and was walking down to the camp to check on his men. Cars he assumed belonged to staff, and which had presumably been under cover in one of the outbuildings, were now scattered around the grounds. At first they looked as if they'd been parked haphazardly until he realised they were strategically placed so there was no chance of a helicopter landing anywhere near the old convent.

In fact, some of the army vehicles also appeared to have been moved, but he'd be better off pretending not to notice. The army had got some good publicity already—if his superiors wanted more, that was too bad.

With the worst behind them, he had stood down most of the soldiers and had again sent the civilians home to catch up on their sleep. From tomorrow on they would all be involved in the clean-up operation, but daylight hours would suffice for that tedious, heart-breaking task.

He had his evening meal with the men, then, satisfied everything was running smoothly, he made his way back to the old building. Should he call in to congratulate Kirsten on her scheme? Would that be sufficient excuse for a visit?

And had she had enough time to cool down?

But as he turned into the corridor that bisected the hospital wing, he knew he couldn't afford the time for a purely social visit to Kirsten no matter how badly he might want to see her.

His time in Murrawarra was limited and a visit to Mr Graham should take priority. His need to know the man better was becoming almost as strong an obsession as his desire to spend time with the doctor.

And both were equally unsettling.

Martin Graham was awake, and he welcomed Harry with the warmth of a man hungry for company. Harry filled him in on what had happened, admitting to a minor error in his plans which had meant one house had taken more water than it need have.

'Overall, I'm fairly satisfied,' he added. 'My main concern now is whether other buildings have been undermined in the same way the council chambers were. I don't want men entering buildings for clean-up work if there's any likelihood of collapse.'

He pulled a map from the back pocket of his trousers and spread it on the bed.

'Look,' he said. 'The contours suggest a depression here, as if perhaps a creek ran down that way towards the river. Did you grow up here?'

The old man nodded.

'Can you remember anything like that?'

Mr Graham shook his head. 'But there are storm-water pipes beneath the main street at about that juncture so perhaps it was a gully down which water ran during heavy rain.'

He pointed to the buildings most likely to be affected. 'Get your engineers to check these out before you start on them.'

His voice was stronger today, his breath less raspy, so Harry encouraged him to participate in planning the clean-up then, oh so casually, introduced more personal questions.

As the older man talked, Harry built up a picture of Martin's life, his loneliness and despair when his city-bred wife had left him to bring up their three-year-old daughter. His determination to do the right thing by Elizabeth.

'My wife vanished so completely I knew she didn't want to be found,' he said, his voice heavy with regret. 'She'd told me as much before she went. Don't try to find me, she'd said, but, of course, I loved her. I had to try.'

Harry felt the heaviness of the man's loss like a cold, hard, jagged lump of metal in his chest.

She loved you, too, he wanted to say, but he didn't know for certain it was true.

'My mistake. Don't wait too long. Don't ever think there are things more important than love.'

The words pierced Harry's thoughts, and he frowned as he tried to make sense of them.

'That was my problem. I was too old—not for her or for love, but for change. Too set in my ways. Too unwilling to look for compromise. The farm was my home, my heritage, my past, my life. I never imagined it couldn't be all of that for her. And if it wasn't, well, I was conceited enough, full enough of confidence and puff, to think that I could more than make up for any shortcomings she might find in being a farmer's wife.'

Harry felt sadness crease his heart, and understanding filter in to ease the baggage he'd carried with him for a long, long time. He admired the man in front of him for having recognised what had happened, and could feel, behind the words, the pain the man had suffered.

'And what now?' Harry asked, although it was the one question he didn't really want answered. 'What of the farm, that heritage?'

Martin sighed.

'Elizabeth loves the place. She'd like to carry it on for one or other of the children, but she's sensible enough to know that all three might drift away—that the pull of the land might not be there for them. And I don't know whether she can do it—a woman on her own—and bring up the children at the same time.'

He looked at Harry.

'I sometimes think that even if I can stay alive to see her through a few more years, I'm more a hindrance than a help to her.'

'I doubt she feels that,' Harry told him. 'And Anthony confided that he doesn't like people dying so, for his sake, you'd better hang in there.'

'He's a good kid,' Martin said, his voice fading as he closed his eyes.

Harry said goodnight and left the room, his uncertainty trailing at his heels like a stray dog.

'Lost in thought or just lost?' Kirsten's voice brought him out of his mental argument. 'Your room's upstairs, first on the left.'

'Have you time to talk? Is it too late? Are you busy?'

He clutched at her shoulders as a drowning man might have clung to his rescuer. He knew his urgency could overwhelm her yet he was unable to tone it down.

She looked up at him, anxiety widening her eyes so they looked huge in the shadowy light.

'Come into my room,' she said, and turned so his hands slid away and were left feeling empty.

'How sick is Martin Graham?' he demanded, as soon as they were shut away behind her door.

He saw the flicker of what looked like disappointment as she reacted to his question but, with the man so weak, that problem had to take priority, no matter what Martin had said about leaving it too late to love.

'He's not so much sick as very frail,' Kirsten replied, recovering her composure so well he had to wonder if he'd imagined that flicker. 'Why?'

Harry was tempted to tell her—to blurt out the whole sorry story—but the caution that was part of his nature had been nurtured and reinforced by the army. He had learned to reconnoitre well before proceeding, and also knew the benefits of an occasional retreat.

'I wondered about shock. If shock can kill people. Frail people. If learning something they may not want or need to know could affect them badly.'

She frowned at him and he wanted more than anything to smooth away that faint crinkle on her brow, but if he touched her he'd forget his purpose.

Forget everything.

'What shock? What is it you want to tell him?' Her brow cleared and her eyes widened again. 'Oh, heavens! You share the same name! Don't tell me you're a long lost son and heir? A child conceived on some wild fling. Not that I can imagine Mr Graham indulging in anything as irresponsible as a wild fling. He's the most proper man on earth. Yes, I can see that could be a shock.'

Harry found himself smiling, more because he now recognised Kirsten's babble of words as her reaction to her own shock.

And recognising reactions was a big step up in any relationship.

Not that they had a relationship.

Or were likely to have one.

Unless.

'Well?' she demanded, coming close enough to poke him again if he wasn't careful. 'Is that what this is all about? Am I right? Is that what you're dithering about asking me? You want to know if telling Mr Graham you're his son will kill him? Is that it?'

Harry stepped back—not so much to avoid her finger but because being close to her made rational thought more difficult.

'It wasn't an irresponsible fling,' he said, focussing his mind on the question even if his body was off on some diversion of its own. 'My mother was his wife, and she was pregnant when she left, although she didn't realise it until later. And then she knew if she told him he'd want to keep me, or at least have contact with me, so she changed her name, left Sydney—where she'd grown up and knew too many people to keep my existence a secret—and started all over again in Victoria.'

'But you're called Graham,' Kirsten objected.

He glared at her.

'You've grasped at the most inessential bit of the whole story,' he complained. 'Of course I'm called Graham, it was my legal name. My mother didn't want that changed, which was totally illogical as she called herself Purvis and I went through life telling lies to my friends to explain the difference in our names.'

'What kind of lies?'

Again the female mind had grasped a very minor point.

'Early on, I said she was an undercover cop who had to change identities, though all my friends knew she worked in a nursing home. And because she never explained the difference to me herself, I assumed she'd remarried when I was too young to remember a man in the house, and that her second husband had died. Of course, if you take that further, because she hadn't told me my father was alive, I'd always assumed he'd died as well, and during those terrible childhood years when imagination runs riot I often wondered if she'd somehow murdered both her husbands.'

'With drugs from the nursing home—of course,' Kirsten murmured.

Harry felt a shiver down his spine. It was exactly how he'd imagined the murders, and he wasn't sure he liked the way Kirsten's thoughts ran in tandem with his. Weird!

'Anyway, all that's in the past. My mother died of cancer

three years ago, and although there was no death-bed con-
fession she left a letter, telling me about my father—also
that I had a sister called Elizabeth—and that she'd loved
Martin Graham but couldn't live his life.'

The words fell into a silence so deep Harry wondered if
Kirsten had heard them.

Until she said, 'I can't see any part of the story so far
that might kill Martin Graham.'

The words were slow-paced, like a lead-in to a song, and
Harry guessed more was coming.

'That's not what's bothering you, is it?' Kirsten asked,
crossing to the window and looking not at him but out into
the darkness. 'Telling the story is the easy part, but can you
give the man a son and not be a son to him? Can you tell
him who you are, meet your sister, acknowledge those three
kids as your blood relatives, then climb into your Land
Rover and ride off into the sunset?'

'It wouldn't have to be like that!' Harry protested, although the damn woman had come close enough to the
truth for him to feel uncomfortable.

She spun back to face him.

'Of course it would. You told me the army is your life.
You're not worried about the effect this news will have on
Martin Graham, you're scared of the effect it will have on
Major Harry. Because you know the family is hurting, and
you'll feel guilty if you tell them who you are then go
blithely back to your own life. So, really, you're saying to
yourself, Wouldn't it be better if they didn't know?'

She stepped close enough to get the finger into action
again.

'Well, you can't dump the decision on me, Harry
Graham, because I'm not going to tell you the shock will
kill your father. In my opinion, finding out he had a son
could add years to the old man's life, but only if that man
was prepared to be a real son—to take on some responsi-

bilities, help Elizabeth run the property, bring up those kids.'

'Listen, you!' Harry said, grabbing the marauding finger and gripping her hand in one of his. 'I'd be worse than useless on a farm. I don't know one end of a cow from the other—and as for kids—'

'Oh, men!' she muttered, snatching her hand away from him and pacing away then back towards him.

'You could learn,' she said, with maddening practicality. 'With cows it's easy. One end bites, and the other end—well, you know what the other end does. And kids aren't that different. They need love and attention—is that so darned hard?'

'I'm in the army!' he stormed, glaring at the infuriating woman striding back and forth in front of him. 'Has that escaped your notice? How can I take care of cows and kids and a sister and an old man when I'm likely to be posted anywhere at a moment's notice? And this is exactly what I've been worrying about. I'd like to have a family, too— even if I don't get to see them often. I'd like to have someone to belong to. But is that selfish? If I can't help them, are they better off not knowing I'm related? I didn't come in here to have you yelling at me about cows. I wanted to talk this thing through.'

'You're the one who's yelling now!' she told him, but he was pleased to see she'd calmed down somewhat. In fact, she was looking at him with a soft expression in her eyes which made his heartbeat go into double time and his head do an about-turn so it was now thinking of how well she'd fitted against his body, not the problem he was so adamant he'd come to discuss.

'I can't help you, Harry,' Kirsten said, her voice soft with regret. 'You know that, don't you? You know it's something you have to decide for yourself. I do agree you can't have everything—but that's life, isn't it? It's all about decisions and compromise, and doing the best we can within the bounds of what's possible.'

He took her in his arms and kissed her, although he knew that was a bad mistake—the worst—because she was an added complication in this impossible equation, but he was reasonably certain that finding a solution to how he felt about her was going to prove even more difficult than reaching a decision about his family.

'We barely know each other,' she murmured between the little kisses he was offering her lips.

'I've three more weeks—longer if I give the troops a break and they don't treat the job with urgency.'

'Not fair on the townspeople hoping to come home,' she murmured, edging her lips towards his ear and flicking her tongue in to punctuate the words.

'Three weeks could be enough.' He was nuzzling at her neck, drinking in the freshness of her skin, the smell of woman that seemed part of some essential essence of her body.

'And then what?'

She pushed herself away—not right away but far enough to look up into his face.

'We're back to decisions, aren't we, Harry? What if we should fall in love? Want more than three weeks?'

'You could be a doctor anywhere,' he reminded her, leaning forward so he could kiss the lids that fluttered down to hide her eyes.

'But not right now,' she said, her eyes opening to show how steely was her core. 'I can't leave Murrawarra at the moment. Not when the fight for the hospital has barely begun. I can't let down these people who welcomed me into their lives, and have made me feel at home. I can't walk away, knowing Moira and Mr Curtis would be transferred to a nursing home in Vereton or, worse still, to the city if beds weren't available locally.'

'So we've got three weeks,' he said, and drew her close again, not for kisses this time but to hold her to his heart while he pondered fate and destiny and love and loss and pain.

It was three weeks of snatched moments, three weeks with the shadow of the decision Harry had to make casting a shadow over their time together. Three weeks when the work of cleaning up a flood-ravaged town continued unabated, when locals trickled back to help and Kirsten found herself busier than ever, patching up the workers' minor injuries.

Yet they managed to see each other almost every day and, although the future wasn't mentioned, Kirsten sometimes hoped that perhaps if Harry fell in love with her it might make his decision easier. Might make him want to stay in Murrawarra.

'It's not only the army versus the family,' he said one day, when they stood above the town and saw the main street water-free. 'It's what I'd do. I couldn't take the farm from Elizabeth, even if I had the skills to run it, which I don't, and although I wouldn't have to work—I've money and a pension—I couldn't not work, Kirsten.'

That million-dollar question—what could Harry do in Murrawarra? It remained unsolved between them, dimming any hopes Kirsten might have harboured that her presence in the town would be enough.

Yet the intensity of their feelings for each other grew until not taking it to an ultimate conclusion seemed pointless.

'Is it like the navy? Do you have a girl in every port? Every town you go to rescue?'

Kirsten asked the question as they lay together in her narrow bed, replete with loving but unable to tear themselves apart, unwilling to waste what precious moments they had left.

He kissed her hair, and rubbed his chin against her head.

'Not quite every port,' he teased, knowing now exactly how to rile her—and delighting in the way the sparks flashed in her eyes.

Except this time it wasn't flashing eyes he received but a sharp jab in the ribs. It made him lose his precarious balance on the edge of the bed so he had to grab at her to stabilise himself. And once she was in his arms again, talk became irrelevant

'Only in Murrawarra,' he amended huskily, his lips pressed against her ear, his body coaxing hers back to heated need.

'Only in Murrawarra,' she repeated, a long time later, and Harry heard the sadness in her voice and knew exactly what she meant.

CHAPTER TWELVE

THE army had been gone for six weeks, and Kirsten dragged herself through each day wondering if, like morning sickness, lovesickness would pass.

True, she'd had postcards from Harry. Of the army base—'Home safely,' it had said. Of towns he'd visited. The dry message, 'We're on manoeuvres.' Several from Sydney, more army barracks or bases or whatever they were called. 'Visited HQ' told her such a lot! There was even one of the Health Department offices, with a note on the back, 'Reconnoitring the enemy's stronghold.'

But the strangest of all, and the one that caused her most anguish, was one from Melbourne. It was a postcard apparently printed for a private hospital, perhaps given to patients in the same way hotels provided stationery.

Kirsten, her heart pounding at the thought that Harry might be ill, turned it over, to find a message even more cryptic than usual.

'Does this give you a clue?' it read, and she frowned over it for ages, eventually going back to the picture of the building, a large and pleasant-looking bungalow set in beautiful gardens, looking more like a private home than a hospital.

She squinted at the ornate sign at the bottom of the drive and just made out the words, 'Purvis Private Hospital'. The name evoked a flash of recognition, too transient to capture, so she turned the card back over and contented herself with brooding over the way Harry formed his words—firm, bold strokes, easy to read. Like the man—the firm and bold part—but easy to read? No way!

'Another love letter?'

Ken came in as she was brooding over it.

'Only if it's written in invisible ink,' she snapped.

'Well, he can hardly write sweet nothings on a postcard, knowing someone on the staff would read it and spread the word.'

'He could put the damn things in envelopes,' Kirsten muttered, then she realised what she'd said and added quickly, 'Not that he's got any reason to write sweet nothings to me!'

'Tell that to the marines!' Ken joked. 'Or should we say "the army"?'

Kirsten turned the conversation to work-related topics. They were back on full staff, the evacuated patients had returned and the hospital was running smoothly. It was also running out of money as the quarter neared an end.

'I'd better speak to all the staff as soon as you can rally them. Perhaps at change of shift. Could you ask everyone going off shift this afternoon to meet in the dining room? I'll explain where we stand to them and then talk to the next shift when they go off duty.'

'Tell them we're closing?' Ken asked, and Kirsten sighed.

'I'll tell them we might have to, unless they're willing to keep working for nothing for a few weeks. I've enough reserves of cash to keep the place running that long.'

'You shouldn't have to do that,' Ken protested. 'It's the administrator's job. I can't believe John Finch has taken stress leave at this time. We're all under stress—especially those of us who stayed here during the floods. And he's pulling his wage and doing sweet nothing!'

'He did try, early on, and he doesn't handle stress well,' Kirsten said, feeling obliged to make excuses for their absent administrator.

She sighed again. 'Martin Graham has always stepped in

and saved things before but he's been so unwell lately, and depressed over having to stay on here instead of going back to the property, that I can't worry him with my problems. And with Jim Thompson still recuperating in town, I don't know where to turn.'

'The staff will work for nothing for a while, but it's not the answer.' Ken pointed out the obvious.

'And shutting down is?' Kirsten snapped, then she apologised for her shortness, sent him on his way and resumed the pacing she'd been doing before the postcard had arrived.

The postcard!

Her reaction to it!

In puzzling over where and what it was, she'd forgotten her first thought. The clue was the hospital. Harry was in hospital. Ill or injured.

She dialled Information and took the short option of being put straight through. When a voice said briskly, 'Purvis Private Hospital,' she realised she didn't know what to say.

'This is Kirsten McPherson,' she began, then, realising a hospital might take more notice of her profession, she amended the introduction to, 'Dr Kirsten McPherson.'

'Yes, Dr McPherson. How may I help you? Do you have a patient with us, or were you wanting information on our services?'

'I wanted—Do you know—? Would a Harry Graham be a patient there?'

There was the click of computer keys then the woman returned. 'No, Doctor, no Harry Graham. Rosevale Private's just up the road—have you tried there?'

Kirsten thanked the woman and hung up. She reached out for the card again and wondered how you brought up messages written in invisible ink.

And sighing didn't help at all.

* * *

By nine o'clock she'd told all but the night staff and those off duty of the dire straits facing the hospital. Unable to remain within the confining walls of the old convent, she walked outside and sat on the bench she and Harry had often shared.

Instead of moonlight shining on the water, there were lights gleaming in the town, squares of paleness where curtains covered windows in the houses, bright flares of streetlights.

Her town, she thought, and sniffed the air, wondering how long it would take for the smell of mud to completely clear away.

Not long, surely, with this hot weather, she thought, for the deluge had given way to summer sun that baked the mud and cracked it into chunks like haphazardly cut slabs of milk chocolate. Even the night was warm, the crickets busy, the moon a taunting yellow lantern in the sky.

'Bother!' she muttered to herself, and, knowing she'd start to feel gloomy if she thought about the moonlight, she looked for something to occupy her time.

The garden and the lawn! She'd looked at it this afternoon and had realised how dry it was getting. After so much rain they'd all assumed it would never need watering again, but she'd need to get the sprinklers going on it if she wanted to keep the grass green.

She walked along close to the building, seeking the main tap at the western corner. Having found it, she turned it on, knowing the timer would automatically switch it off an hour later. A yell of anger from around the side startled her.

A familiar yell?

Surely not.

She hurried around the corner and saw the still protesting visitor, standing wet and dripping, under the lights at the entrance to the hospital wing.

Only this time he was in jeans and a knit shirt, which clung just as lovingly as wet fatigues to the flat planes and sculpted muscle of his chest.

'What the hell do you think you're doing, woman?' he yelled at her. 'You nearly drowned me.'

'Welcome back,' Kirsten managed to get out in between bursts of laughter and silent admonitions to her heart to remain calm. Harry could just be passing through. 'Come to buy a postcard of Murrawarra to send to someone in another port?'

'That's what I should do!' he retorted, flapping his arms to get rid of the water trickling down from his hair. 'A man must be mad to get involved with this place!'

'Why don't you get into some dry clothes?' Kirsten suggested, smiling because she couldn't help herself. Just seeing him again was filling her with joy. 'You're usually much better tempered when you're dry.'

'You little—' he began, then he, too, smiled—and moved towards her, holding out his arms, so it seemed natural to step into their sheltering arc and tuck her body hard against his.

'We'll both be wet,' he murmured when the first heated kiss had stolen so much breath they'd had to break apart or faint from lack of oxygen.

'I don't care,' she told him, snuggling closer so at least the dampness was warm from body heat.

She lifted her head for another breath-defying kiss.

'Aren't you going to ask why I'm here?' he asked, when they paused again.

Kirsten snuggled even closer.

'I don't seem to care about that either,' she muttered, content just to remain in his arms.

This time she kissed him, initiating the touch of mouth to mouth, the exploratory moves of tongue on tongue.

She'd decided kisses weren't enough and was wondering

what the full complement of staff would think if she dragged him down the corridor to her room when he eased himself away again, and with his hands on her shoulders, holding her steady, he said, 'We need to talk. I want to explain, but first I need to see my father. Is he still here? Or was he well enough to leave?'

I need to see my father. The simple sentence told Kirsten most of what she wanted to know. Her heart began a mad cavorting in her chest and the quivers were so bad she wondered she could stay upright without support.

'He's still here,' she began, then realised how late it was and looked up into Harry's dark eyes. 'In the morning would be better. I know you can't want to wait, having come all this way to see him—having decided—but he's—'

Harry stopped her with a finger to her lips, and a smile that made her think the sun had suddenly come out.

'Frail,' he finished gently. 'Yes, I know. I dumped my kit at the motel. I'll come back in the morning.'

He drew her close again.

'Dry,' he added in her ear, and she could tell he was still smiling.

But he was also telling her that was all for now. Telling her she must wait. And while most of her understood—for in telling his father who he was he would be rediscovering himself—she was human enough to want more.

She could feel his lips teasing in her hair, his hands warm on her back, and she smoothed her fingers across the wetness of his shirt and tried to make them tell him how she felt.

'I love you, Kirsten,' he whispered into her curls. 'You do know that, don't you?'

Do I?

'And everything will be all right,' he continued, without waiting for her answer. 'With the hospital, the town, Elizabeth and the farm. I'll need to learn so much, to feel my way, but…' he eased her back again and looked down into her face '…with you by my side I could move mountains, pretty doctor. Will you be there for me? Stand beside me? Let me join your battles, be your ally? Perhaps, in time, be more than that?'

And although the words were those of reassurance, his voice became uncertain so Kirsten had to kiss him again to answer, at the least, the last of his questions.

'If I don't go now, I'll never go,' he warned her, when she broke off to take a breath.

And much as she wanted to opt for the 'never', she knew it would be wrong.

'I'll see you in the morning,' she said, then, unable to be parted quite so quickly, walked down the hill with him, past the grassy slope where, not so long ago, the mushroom tents had sprouted in the rain.

Harry came at eight next morning and spent the day with Martin Graham. Kirsten took in snacks and meals herself, leaving the trays and walking out again, unwilling to intrude lest she disturb the delicate balance on the tightrope of emotions the two men must be walking.

At five, Harry emerged, almost grey with fatigue.

'You'd better see to him,' he said to Kirsten. 'I didn't want to exhaust him but I couldn't leave. There's so much to say, to learn about each other. I find I need him, Kirsten, just as much as he needs me.'

Kirsten put her arms around the man she loved and held him close for a moment.

'Go upstairs,' she suggested. 'Now we're back to normal staffing, I'm sleeping in the room you had. Have a rest there. I'll come up later.'

He nodded and moved away, either too exhausted or too emotionally wrung out to argue with her.

In Martin's room, Kirsten took her patient's pulse,

checked his blood pressure, listened to his breathing and said nothing. The old man needed time and rest.

'I'd like to put you on the respirator overnight,' she suggested, but he shook his head.

'I'll take it easy. Use the oxygen when I need it.' Then he took Kirsten's hand. 'He says he doesn't want the farm, but he'll give Elizabeth any help she needs. Do we believe him, Kirsten? Can we take all this on trust?'

Kirsten thought carefully before she answered.

'That's something you have to decide,' she said. 'But from what I know of him, he has so many of your fine qualities that I'd be inclined to believe him. Not that it matters, because you can tie up the farm in such a way that it goes to Elizabeth and the children.'

Martin Graham looked shocked at the suggestion.

'And cut my own son out of my will?' he spluttered.

Kirsten smiled at him.

'Haven't you just answered your own question?' she said gently. 'And anyway, now's not the time to talk of wills or anything so far into the future. I have it on excellent authority he doesn't know one end of a cow from the other—which won't matter much as you run sheep, not cows. But if he's to be any use to Elizabeth you'd better stick around for a while to teach him the basics.'

She saw the glimmer of a smile around the old man's lips, and as he closed his eyes and drifted off to sleep she wondered if the day's emotions hadn't taken far more out of Harry than they had out of his father.

An hour later, she was done—off duty unless called for an emergency. She went upstairs, thinking of a shower, a change of clothes—Harry had never seen her dressed in anything but work clothes—then perhaps they could have dinner downtown in one of the town's two post-flood renovated restaurants.

She opened the door quietly in case he was sleeping, but

he was sitting on her bed, studying the postcards he'd sent, which she'd ranged in order along the wall above her desk.

He smiled at her and patted the bed, and when she sat down beside him, he put his arm around her shoulders and held her close.

'Did you work it out?' he asked, still smiling.

'Work what out?' she demanded. 'Your stupid messages, or the invisible ink? If you'd told me you were in the secret service, I might have tried.'

'I love it when you're fiery,' he said, and dropped a kiss on her nose. 'No, the postcards. No secret ink—the pictures!'

Kirsten studied them again.

Holdsworthy Base—his first stop after Murrawarra. The big barracks and some other cards from Sydney. The Health Department one, and the private hospital.

Which reminded her.

'That last one sent me crazy!' she said, turning so she could pummel him gently in the ribs. 'I thought it meant you were in hospital. I even rang them up to ask how you were, what had happened to you. And they said you weren't a patient but to try some place down the road.'

'Rosevale Private, its opposition, and the girl on the switchboard wouldn't have connected a request for information on a patient called Harry Graham with me—even if she'd known my name.'

'What on earth are you talking about?' Kirsten demanded, stopping the pummelling and rubbing her fingers across his chest instead.

He stood up and plucked the final postcard from the wall, then handed it to her.

'Read the sign,' he said.

'I've read it,' Kirsten told him. 'It says, ''Purvis Private Hospital''. That's why I panicked, you stupid man!'

'And it didn't ring a bell?' he persisted.

Kirsten frowned. It *had* rung a bell, but she hadn't caught the flash of recognition quickly enough to track it down.

'I've heard the name,' she said cautiously, and the infuriating man she loved grinned at her.

'I told you it,' he said smugly. 'It was my mother's name.'

'Should all this mean something to me?' she demanded. 'Are you telling me this was the name of the man your mother murdered and he owned the nursing home?'

Harry gave a great shout of laughter and sat down so he could scoop his edgy, tetchy, thoroughly confused darling into his arms.

'The murders only existed in my imagination, but the hospital is real enough. My mother was a nurse. She founded it. She persuaded a group of businessmen and doctors to put money into excellence and they provided the backing. It's now run by a company with competent business and medical administrators and has three sister hospitals—are hospitals female, do you suppose? Anyway, possibly soon it will have four.'

The tetchy darling detached herself very deliberately from his arms and rose to her full five feet five.

'Are you telling me you own four private hospitals?' she demanded. 'That your mother left Martin, changed her name, took herself to Melbourne and founded not just one but four private hospitals?'

'Not all at once,' he said hurriedly, although he wasn't quite sure why this news was so upsetting to Kirsten. 'And, in fact, the fourth one we've bought since she died. She'd been negotiating for it when she became ill so it seemed the only thing to do.'

'We've bought?' she echoed. 'You're involved in those decisions?'

'Well, I'm a shareholder and I'm on the board. I don't know much about the medical things, but the administrators brief the board.' Harry spoke apologetically, aware that the way he'd planned to say all this wasn't working out. Also aware that his other plans, which had included a long night of loving, were fading fast.

'I *can* follow simple logic and do know some business principles,' he pointed out, 'though why the hell I'm justifying myself to you I don't know. I thought you'd be pleased!'

'Pleased you own a string of private hospitals?' Kirsten spat out, so enraged she could barely speak. 'So you could bestow on me a job should I ever need one, I suppose.'

The scathing tones suggested long nights of loving couldn't have been further from her mind.

'I thought you'd come back because you were going to stay in Murrawarra,' she continued. 'Help Elizabeth on the farm, be an uncle to her kids, a son to your father. I'd even thought you might help me save the hospital, but if you've already got four of your own a little operation like Murrawarra can't mean much to you.'

Harry raised his eyes to heaven, then heaved himself to his feet, grabbed the little termagant by the shoulders and gave her a gentle shake.

'Will you stop jumping to conclusions, shut those lovely lips for a moment, and let me explain?'

He reached out and took the first postcard off the wall.

'My base,' he said. 'I saw my commanding officer and explained I wanted out of the army for family reasons.'

'But the army's your—' Kirsten began, and he silenced her with a kiss.

'The army *was* my life,' he corrected her, his hands gentler now, stroking her body and firing sensations that made it difficult for Kirsten to focus on the next postcard he held out to her.

'The headquarters in Sydney where my discharge is being sorted out.'

He kissed her again, although she was too tense with wanting him to argue any more.

'The Health Department where I've been arguing with bureaucrats about joint ventures between private and public hospitals, about private hospitals taking public patients on a "government pays" basis which will work out cheaper for the government than running smaller hospitals themselves.'

Kirsten looked at him, certain the relief she felt must be shining in her eyes.

'You can save the hospital?' she asked.

He smiled at her.

'Is that all you have to ask? Is that your only concern?'

She felt the frown lines creasing her forehead and remembered another worry she'd had about Harry and Murrawarra.

'But what will *you* do?' she asked.

He grinned at her.

'You mean when I'm not learning farming from my father, or doing dogsbody work out on the farm for my sister, or being an uncle to the kids, or checking on the running of my latest acquisition, and the continued operations of the other four?'

Harry rubbed his chin, and mischief gleamed like golden candles in his eyes.

'I guess I could make love to my girlfriend, perhaps get married. Have some kids so Anthony, Meg and Libby could have cousins. What do you think?'

Kirsten stood on tiptoe and kissed him on the lips.

'How soon could we start on the first part of that suggestion?' she whispered, and heard his laughter echo around the little room as he took her in his arms and swung her in the air.

MILLS & BOON®

Makes any time special™

Mills & Boon publish 29 new titles every month. Select from...

Modern Romance™   Tender Romance™

Sensual Romance™

Medical Romance™   Historical Romance™

MAT2

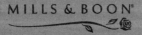

4 Books
and a surprise gift!

We would like to take this opportunity to thank you for reading this Mills & Boon® book by offering you the chance to take FOUR more specially selected titles from the Medical Romance™ series absolutely FREE! We're also making this offer to introduce you to the benefits of the Reader Service™—

★ FREE home delivery
★ FREE gifts and competitions
★ FREE monthly Newsletter
★ Books available before they're in the shops
★ Exclusive Reader Service discounts

Accepting these FREE books and gift places you under no obligation to buy; you may cancel at any time, even after receiving your free shipment. Simply complete your details below and return the entire page to the address below. *You don't even need a stamp!*

YES! Please send me 4 free Medical Romance books and a surprise gift. I understand that unless you hear from me, I will receive 6 superb new titles every month for just £2.49 each, postage and packing free. I am under no obligation to purchase any books and may cancel my subscription at any time. The free books and gift will be mine to keep in any case.

M1ZEB

Ms/Mrs/Miss/Mr ....Initials ....
BLOCK CAPITALS PLEASE

Surname...

Address...

....

....Postcode ....

Send this whole page to:
UK: The Reader Service, FREEPOST CN81, Croydon, CR9 3WZ
EIRE: The Reader Service, PO Box 4546, Kilcock, County Kildare (stamp required)

Offer not valid to current Reader Service subscribers to this series. We reserve the right to refuse an application and applicants must be aged 18 years or over. Only one application per household. Terms and prices subject to change without notice. Offer expires 31st August 2001. As a result of this application, you may receive further offers from Harlequin Mills & Boon Limited and other carefully selected companies. If you would prefer not to share in this opportunity please write to The Data Manager at the address above.

Mills & Boon® is a registered trademark owned by Harlequin Mills & Boon Limited.
Medical Romance™ is being used as a trademark.